Truth or Fashion

THE INTERNS NOVELS
by Chloe Walsh

Book One: *Fashionistas*
Book Two: *Truth or Fashion*

Chloe Walsh

the INTERNS
Truth or Fashion

HARPER TEEN

An Imprint of HarperCollins*Publishers*

HarperTeen is an imprint of HarperCollins Publishers.

Truth or Fashion

Copyright © 2008 by HarperCollins Publishers

www.harperteen.com

Library of Congress catalog card number: 2008924433
ISBN 978-0-06-137089-2

Typography by Amy Ryan

First Edition

Truth or Fashion

"The fairy smiled. With a flick of her magic wand, Cinderella found herself wearing the most beautiful dress, the loveliest ever seen in the realm."

Filed under: Fashionista > Style

Here's some food for fashion thought: Would Cinderella have wowed her prince without that glam gown and those adorable slippers, compliments of her fairy godmother? Does the outfit make the girl? Or does the girl make the outfit?

The Fashionista has been musing about transformations lately. In part, because she's witnessed some remarkable turnarounds. There's that <u>troubled socialite,</u> for instance, who found God overnight, and now wears a red <u>Kabala</u> »

<u>bracelet</u> and walks around bragging about her newfound inner peace (as if a string bracelet and a big mouth make her the <u>Dalai Lama</u>). Then there's that wannabe fashion designer whose naked ambition has turned her into the worst kind of liar (I suspect that those with true talent needn't sacrifice their integrity for success). But my favorite is that Plain Jane, who the Fashionista witnessed at last weekend's <u>*Couture* Cutting Edge Gala</u>. That girl was positively transformed into what can only be described as a fairy princess.

Of course, a transformation doesn't guarantee a fairy-tale ending. We all need more than a dress (or a piece of red string, or great big ambitions) to achieve happily ever after. The elements of happiness—like the separate pieces of a perfectly constructed outfit—require style, creativity, and a dash of magical alchemy. Guaranteeing happy endings is unfortunately beyond the realm of the Fashionista's control, but I can definitely be of assistance when it comes to matters of style. Just call me your fashion fairy godmother.

Your faithful Fashionista

1

All-out Fashion War

CALLIE RYAN STOOD IN THE immense marble lobby of
Conrad Media's office tower, summoning the courage
to push through the turnstiles and on up to the offices
of *Couture* magazine. The trip to the thirty-third floor
was nothing new to her. She'd made it every weekday
for the last six weeks. And after half a summer interning at *Couture*, Callie no longer felt cowed when she
entered the mag's white, modernist lobby, even as the
famous face of the latest cover girl stared down at her
from a six-foot blow-up. (Scarlett last month. Beyoncé
now.) In fact, for the past several weeks, Callie had
started each day with the most delicious feeling that she

3

was shedding her Midwestern girl persona and becoming a true New Yorker. She'd felt on the verge of becoming One of Them.

But this particular Monday morning, she was on the verge of something else entirely—a date with a firing squad. Well, it wasn't that bad. The *Couture* Cutting Edge Gala had just happened three days ago, and as far as the magazine staff was concerned, Callie was still the seventeen-year-old wunderkind designer from Columbus, Ohio, who'd swept into New York and quickly landed her original handbag designs in the top fashion magazine in the country. But Callie had a secret. She'd taken credit for the silk screens that she'd used to create her handbags, and the silk-screen artist—a cute but seriously ticked-off designer from Brooklyn named Quinn McGrath—was threatening to expose her as a fake.

"Hey, girl, you lose something?" The brassy voice of one of Callie's fellow interns, Nadine Van Buren, called after her through the marble lobby. Callie looked at Nadine, dressed outlandishly as usual in a fuchsia Michael Kors buttoned minidress. She was coiffed in a Louise Brooks black bobbed wig, and her feet were arched to the extreme in a pair of silver lamé platform heels that almost made tiny Nadine look tall.

"Um, not really," Callie replied. "Just looking for my ID," she said, fumbling through the vintage Chanel crocodile handbag she'd bought a few weeks ago at the Chelsea Flea Market. The thing was beyond beat-up, but at least Callie could now say she owned a bona fide Chanel. Ever since coming to New York, she'd felt like her non-designer clothes and accessories weren't up to snuff and she'd sunk into a bit of debt to repair that. Today she'd paired the bag with a white linen H&M sundress—tag torn out to hide its low-budget provenance—and a charcoal jacket that she'd made herself.

"Oh, don't worry," Nadine reassured Callie. "The guard knows me. Don't you, Raul, my man?" Nadine winked at Raul as she stepped brazenly through the turnstile. All he could do was blush as he watched her sashay all the way to the elevator bank. Then he turned to Callie and waved her through, too. *So much for stalling,* Callie thought as she followed Nadine into the elevator.

"You seem chipper," she noted, looking Nadine over. "Feeling better?" Callie knew firsthand how much her roommate liked to party. The girl had spent more of her time this summer boozing with Aynsley Rothwell—rich Upper East Side socialite, fellow *Couture* intern, unbearable snob—than she had shooting pictures or researching articles. And at the gala, Nadine had outdone herself. She'd then spent most of Saturday in their shared New York University dorm room, hiding under the covers with the shades drawn—until she slunk off to Aynsley's town house just before dinner.

"I'm fine," Nadine insisted. "I just need a little extra hangover therapy, if you know what I mean. That was some party. And did you see the Fashionista blog about the gala? Ava got a mention! Can you friggin' believe it?"

Callie could believe it. Her friend Ava Barton had been the hands-down belle of the ball—a major coup for an intern.

As the elevator doors opened and Beyoncé's luminous face smiled down at Callie, Nadine appraised the cover. "Damn, all that chick's got on me is a few inches. I'm just as hot as she is, don't you think?"

Callie was equal parts dismayed and impressed by Nadine's typical bravado. No matter how much trouble she got into, she swaggered around like she owned the place. Callie wished she had some of that boldness. Then again, it was a combo of boldness and ambition that had led to the trouble concerning Quinn's silk screens.

"Good morning, ladies," squeaked *Couture*'s main receptionist. "Staffwide meeting in the conference room. Isabel wants everyone there. Fifteen minutes."

"Isabel" was Isabel Dupre, the glamorous and powerful editor in chief of *Couture*. It was Isabel who'd given Callie her big break when she'd selected her handbags to be in the magazine's Cutting Edge Designer Showcase issue. A woman like Isabel had the ability to launch Callie's career—or kill it. Two days ago, Callie had been hoping for the former, but now that Isabel was about to discover the truth about Callie's creations, she feared that career death was a more likely outcome.

"I'd better call Sly," Nadine whispered. "She's running late."

What else is new? Callie thought. Aynsley "Sly" Rothwell treated her internship like a hobby. *No*—it was worse than that. She acted like she was doing everyone a huge favor every time she deigned to show up. She seemed to think that having as much money as a Trump and a wardrobe to rival *Couture*'s sample closet meant she could come and go as she pleased. As far as Callie was concerned, the only good thing about Aynsley Rothwell was her brother, Julian—all six dark, sexy, smoldering feet of him.

Callie padded through the hallways, dodging rolling racks of angular suits, trench coats, and equestrian pants—all the must-have items for fall—and slid into the intern office. No one else was there, so she quickly logged on to her computer and glanced at her emails. There was one from Julian, congratulating her on her big gala night and asking her out this coming Friday. That put a smile on her face—until the next message, from Quinn McGrath, made her stomach tense into a ball. Reluctantly, she clicked it open.

Hello Callie:

Now that the gala's over, time to come clean. We should talk this week, and I suggest you set up a meeting for you, me, and your editors for sometime next week, so that we can sort through this fiasco.

Q. Mc

"Good morning, Cal!" Callie turned around to find Ava, the one person she actually trusted, beaming a thousand-watt smile her way. All weekend long Callie had wanted to tell Ava her secret, but after the gala, all Ava seemed to do was gush about how great it had all been, and then on Saturday she'd skedaddled off to her parents' house on Long Island for the rest of the weekend. Callie quickly closed Quinn's message and stood up to hug her friend.

"Hey, you okay?" Ava asked as Callie clung to her.

"I'm fine. Just so excited about the gala and everything," Callie lied. "Congratulations, Ava—I mean about the Fashionista mention, and all."

"Thanks. I'm still aglow," Ava replied. And she looked it. With her long brown hair, almond-shaped brown eyes, and adorable dimples, Ava had always been pretty enough. But she'd never had the confidence that is every girl's best accessory— until the night of the gala, that is. That night, she'd been so positively radiant in her Elie Saab couture gown that people had mistaken her for a model or a starlet. And some of the magic of that evening had clearly carried over, because today, even in her old Banana Republic halter dress with beaded Calypso sandals, she looked uncharacteristically glamorous.

"Ready to hit the meeting?" Ava asked.

Callie swallowed back the pit in her throat. Quinn hadn't spilled the beans; she had no reason to be worried. But still, she was. She nodded and followed Ava down the hall, past the glass double doors, and into the conference room. The cadre of sharp-looking editors perfectly turned out in Balenciaga, Armani, and Zac Posen turned to Ava and smiled—more proof of her transformation. As Callie and Ava took their seats at the steel-and-glass conference table, Nadine flounced in with a haughty look on her face that seemed to dare the editors to show her any attitude. Five seconds after that, Aynsley strode through the door, her tar-black hair sloping over her dark eyes. She was wearing a black-and-gray leopard-print Alessandro Dell'Acqua that Callie had positively coveted when she'd seen it in *Couture* a few months back. Of course, the dress cost as much as her parents' mortgage payment, so covet was about all she could do.

Next, Kiki Benedict, *Couture*'s deputy editor, waltzed in, followed by Dieter Glück, the stone-faced creative director. Isabel's assistant arrived soon after, bearing a bone china cup brimming with cappuccino, which she set at the head of the table. The staff grew quiet. Then in strode Isabel, her chic black spiky hair looking extra threatening, her white Gucci suit showing off her size two bod. Callie wondered how someone so tiny could seem so huge. Power did that, she supposed.

"*Bonjour, bonjour,*" Isabel trilled. "*Oh, là, là.* That was some party we had, *non?*" She dropped a stack of papers on the table: the *New York Post* and *Daily News* had covered the gala in their gossip pages. So had Gawker, Gothamist, and Mediabistro. "And did you read what the Fashionista wrote about us? I think we should take a moment to toast our success. To Dieter and Kiki and their staffs for creating our most visionary Cutting Edge showcase so far. *Brava!*" The staff applauded. Dieter looked unmoved. Kiki feigned embarrassment.

"Also, we must raise our glasses to the interns who helped plan the event." Isabel raised her china cup and a parade of Poland Spring bottles and sweaty iced Starbucks concoctions followed. "Two of our girls really stood out. Ava embodied the next generation of *Couture* women: smart, accomplished, and gorgeously dressed. And Callie—who will no doubt dress the next generation—was a fabulous publicity peg. Our teenage designer! *Mon dieu.* Marc Jacobs had better watch his back!"

Isabel laughed and then trained her violet eyes on Nadine and Aynsley. "I think some people in this room might take a lesson from Ava and Callie," she said, her eyebrows arched. Callie watched as Nadine's mocha skin flushed a deep red. Aynsley, however, sat perfectly still, that smirky smile of hers not budging an inch, even though Callie knew she was in some serious hot water. Aynsley was supposed to have been manning the door the night of the gala, making sure all those socialite friends of hers got into the party. Instead, she'd let Nadine in, and then abandoned her post. *Typical,* Callie thought. *There isn't an ounce of work ethic in that slouchy, skinny body of hers!*

"*Décorez,*" Isabel continued. "The gala is the good news. Unfortunately, we have some very bad news, as well, which is going to translate into a lot of work for us all."

From the pile of newspapers, Isabel extracted a copy of *Style* magazine and held it before them. *Style* was one of *Couture*'s inferior competitors. "This is an advance copy of their next issue," she said in her most commanding editor-in-chief voice. The cover featured Victoria Beckham wearing a periwinkle dress that looked familiar, but Callie didn't get what the big deal was. Whatever Isabel was building up to, in Callie's mind it couldn't possibly have been as bad as the news she and Quinn were about to spill.

At the mere sight of Posh, Dieter, Kiki, and several other staffers gasped in horror. Callie shot a quizzical look toward Ava, who was looking even more horrified than Kiki. Then Callie instantly remembered why

Victoria's dress looked familiar—it was the same design Ava had "borrowed" from the sample closet to wear on a date several weeks ago.

"For those of you who don't know," Isabel continued, "Victoria is wearing a beautiful Alexander McQueen gown—*the very same gown* that Kirsten Dunst is wearing on our October cover." Isabel shuddered. "Obviously, we cannot have people thinking that we're following in *Style*'s footsteps. Perhaps this is all a terrible mistake—but it is the third time in as many months that a feature planned for *Couture* has wound up in *Style* first. One time is a coincidence. Twice is unfortunate. Three times is espionage."

The entire conference room erupted in a roar as staffers panicked. Callie knew this was a big deal, a serious problem, but she was so wrapped up in her own worries that she had trouble taking it all in. She looked at the other interns. Aynsley was still smirking, acting like she found the pandemonium endlessly amusing. Nadine was staring daggers at Nelson, the copy chief. Then Callie turned to Ava, who looked like she might cry. *But why so upset?* Callie thought. Sure, Ava had borrowed that dress from the sample closet, but she'd also returned it with no one but Callie the wiser. Really, the only thing Ava was guilty of was having exquisite taste. After all, she'd borrowed the one dress that both *Couture* and *Style* had anointed The Look for fall.

Isabel clapped her hands and the room immediately quieted. "Don't worry. We won't be caught with our pants down. We are investigating the source of the leak but, as we hunt for the spy, we are ripping up the entire October issue and starting from scratch—this time, taking extra precautions. Section editors will be divided into teams and will report only to Kiki, Dieter, or me. We will approve all new layouts and content and have an expedited schedule to make our press deadline. There will be no more staffwide meetings, no public production or shoot schedules. The sample closet will be locked. Everything must be kept top-secret until the issue goes to press in four weeks."

The conference room was now complete bedlam. To tear up an issue that had taken months to plan and remake it in a matter of weeks was a near-impossible feat. But Isabel looked serene in the face of all the chaos, as if she planned to enjoy the massive undertaking.

"*Chers,* calm down. A little hard work never hurt anyone. Just think of yourselves as part of the French resistance movement. We're outsmarting the Germans." Isabel scanned the room with her penetrating eyes. When she spoke again, her voice had dropped an octave and her smile had vanished. "And don't underestimate the seriousness of this situation, *mes chers*. What we are engaged in is nothing less than an all-out fashion war."

2

Kmart meets Jimmy Choo

AS THE *COUTURE* STAFFERS filed out of the meeting in shock, Kiki yelled to Callie, Ava, Aynsley, and Nadine, "In my office. Now," eliciting an ever-so-subtle eye roll from Aynsley. Nadine could tell her friend thought this whole spy business was nothing more than a juicy piece of gossip. But for Nadine it represented something else: her salvation.

She'd first overheard the editors discussing the possibility of a *Couture* spy a few weeks ago, and she'd determined then that she was going to solve the mystery. Back in Philadelphia, she'd been the editor in chief of her high school newspaper. She'd had two articles published in *Seventeen*. She was going to Penn next year. Nadine Van Buren might have a body to die for and the chutzpah to show it off, but she also had a brain. She'd been a little off her game since arriving in New York—so many bars, so many boys, so little time. But finding the *Couture* mole was a golden opportunity to prove her reporting talents and get off the *Couture* shit list once and for all.

"You coming, Van Buren?" Aynsley asked.

"You go ahead," Nadine replied. "I'm gonna hang back a bit."

"Okay, Nancy Drew," Aynsley said with a smirk.

Nadine smirked right back at her. Aynsley could be a bitch, but if you knew how to handle the girl, she was like putty. Nadine pressed her ear against the side of the conference room door. Kiki, Dieter, and Isabel were still inside, speaking in hushed tones. Nadine had her suspicions about Dieter; she thought he might be gunning for Isabel's job, even though Aynsley claimed that was ridiculous. Aynsley liked to act like she knew everything about the fashion industry, and yes, the girl seemed to have as much knowledge about designers as Kiki and Dieter combined, but then again, Aynsley was also on the verge of being shipped off to Italy to spend the rest of the summer under the strict supervision of her parents. Nadine knew that *Couture* was Aynsley's last chance to prove herself before her rich parents pulled the plug on her charmed lifestyle—and she wasn't exactly a model employee.

Never mind what Aynsley thought—Dieter wasn't Nadine's number-one suspect anyway. That was a tie between the copy chief, Nelson, and a cranky fashion editor named Chiara.

The door swung open, nearly taking Nadine's wig off with it. Isabel and Dieter whipped by. Kiki eyed her viciously. "Eavesdropping?" she asked.

"Um, no. Just waiting for you, wondering how I can help out." Nadine did her best to sound sincere. Kiki had been riding her ass in the worst way the last few weeks, and to say that Nadine resented the blond deputy editor was like saying that New York was a big town.

"Trust me, we've got everything under control," Kiki trilled. "Now come on."

Nadine followed Kiki back to her office, where Callie and Ava sat waiting patiently on her black leather couch. Aynsley lounged to their left in a Mies van der Rohe Barcelona chair. As Kiki took a seat behind her desk, Nadine made her way over to the couch and sandwiched herself between Ava and Callie.

"Well, you're either the luckiest interns we've ever had or the most cursed," Kiki said, with an amused snarl playing on her lips. "As you know, we are axing the entire October feature well, plus most of the front-of-book pieces. Isabel seems to feel that the best way to outsmart *Style* is to think entirely outside the box, so she wants all of *you* to submit concepts to replace what would have been a ten-page piece on vintage influences in evening wear. You'll be working in teams of two; you'll have ten days to submit a concept, a full proposal, pitch package, and storyboard. If either team's idea is worthy, it'll go in the magazine. If neither is worthy, you're all fired." Kiki laughed. "Just kidding. Just think of it as a contest. The winner will get some fab yet-to-be-determined perk. The loser will get a double dose of humiliation."

Nadine saw Ava and Callie shoot each other a smile—the cocky bitches obviously assumed they'd win—and Kiki caught their sly exchange, too. "By all rights, we *should* pair Callie with Ava and Nadine with Aynsley," Kiki said. "After all, Callie and Ava have stepped up like superstars around here, with Callie's bag making the Cutting Edge Showcase and Ava's editorial work earning her a byline." Nadine looked up to see Ava smiling shyly, while Callie—who usually sucked up the spotlight like a supermodel—was bash-fully staring at her feet.

"But the other half of you," Kiki continued, staring at Nadine and Aynsley, "well, let's just say that your lackluster performance is beyond disappointing. Alas, this little contest is *not* about justice; it's about success—*Couture*'s success. So we can't handicap ourselves by loading one team with fashion delinquents and the other team with talent. That would be like accessorizing a Kmart dress with orthopedic shoes." Kiki shriveled her nose in distaste. "You make a bad thing worse. Instead, we'll take the Kmart dresses—Aynsley and Nadine—and pair them with fabulous Jimmy Choos—Callie and Ava. We'll mix up the teams!" she said triumphantly.

It took Nadine a minute to untangle Kiki's metaphor. Was she really comparing her and Aynsley to ugly shoes and cheap dresses? What a bitch. But the insult also meant that Nadine would be working with Ava and Aynsley would be toiling away with Callie—so Kiki had actually just done Nadine a major favor. Ava was a workhorse. The girl had no life. She didn't even date—though, after having caught Ava in the midst of a cozy afternoon lunch with an older hottie several weeks ago, Nadine had *thought* she was having

20

an affair. It turned out that the Silver Fox was just some designer named Kain Ellis, whom Ava had interviewed for a *Couture* feature. And, to prove Nadine's point even further, Ava's article had been good enough to earn her a byline in the magazine. The girl was a genius!

Between Ava's work ethic and Nadine's natural sense of style, Nadine was convinced that the two of them would do a kick-ass job. Sly might be the dishiest of the fashion plates, with a half dozen hot designers on speed dial, but the girl was as lazy as her hedge-fund daddy was loaded. And as for Callie, she was a good enough designer, sure, but she and Aynsley were like two alpha chicks gunning for top dog status. The pure entertainment potential of a daily Callie-Aynsley standoff was almost too delicious to imagine. Nadine sneaked a glance at Aynsley, who, oddly, was looking as pleased about the assignment as Nadine was. In fact, Aynsley looked like the cat that swallowed the canary.

"So, you have until the middle of next week, which means you've all got your work cut out for you," Kiki said with a chuckle. "*We all do.* Any questions?"

"Um, do you want us to include our own designs?" Callie began.

"Callie, much as we treasure your creative input,

what we're looking for here is an overall concept—like hot fur trends or Asian influences. And as for designers, stick to established names rather than falling back on your own creations, okay? I'll want your finished proposals by next Wednesday, so off you go. I expect to be wildly impressed."

The interns filed out of Kiki's office, all of them except Aynsley apparently struck dumb by the enormity of their assignment.

"Do you want to meet in the small conference room?" Ava whispered to Nadine.

"Sure. Why don't I go grab us a couple of lattes and I'll meet you there in a sec."

On her way toward the lobby, Nadine pulled Aynsley aside. "Damn, I wish we were working together," she lied.

"Oh, me too. But I'm sure it'll all work out for the best," Aynsley trilled insincerely. Nadine obviously wasn't the only one bullshitting.

Nadine bought two Frappuccinos from Starbucks and made her way upstairs to the small conference room. Ava had already spread out the last three October *Couture*s on the table, alongside issues of *Style*, *Vogue*, *Elle*, and *Bazaar*. "I thought we'd take a look at what everyone else has been doing so that we can do something completely different," she explained.

"Sounds like a plan," Nadine said reassuringly. "But I think we should also focus on what we both personally find inspiring. I mean most of *Couture*'s editors never leave New York—it's like they're all breathing the same stale air. Whereas *we* both bring a fresh perspective."

"Which is to say we're novices," Ava added.

"That's right. We *are* novices, but in a way that's gonna help us kick ass," Nadine insisted. "We can think outside of the box much better than these uptight fashion bitches."

"That's certainly true," said a male voice from the hallway. "If anyone could liven things up around here, it would be you two."

As soon as Nadine recognized the voice as that of *Couture*'s staff photographer, Sam Owens, she wanted to jump underneath the table. She had done some pretty outrageous things around guys in the past, but nothing quite as crazy as what had happened in the car on her way home from the gala with Sam. It hurt just thinking about it.

Sam was so hot—with his black hair, laughter-filled blue eyes, and effortless punky-preppy style, not to mention his sexy British accent. He'd been so nice to

Nadine. She assumed he was into her, but then, when she'd tried to seduce him at the gala, Sam had brushed her off. And that was *before* she'd done the unthinkable—puked all over him in the car, when he'd so gallantly offered to see her home. Then, instead of kicking her to the curb, he'd carried her up to her room and put her to bed, where he could've easily taken advantage of her. But, as Nadine's luck would have it, he'd been a perfect gentleman. Probably because he found her as appealing as yesterday's sushi.

"Hi, Sam," Ava said. "We're brainstorming a new concept for a feature."

"So I gathered. Actually, Marceline filled me in on the big intern competition. Apparently, it's supposed to be top-secret, but there are enough loose lips around here to sink a battalion's worth of ships."

Nadine pretended to concentrate on a *Vogue* layout. She was dying to look at Sam, but she couldn't bring herself to meet his eyes.

"It's such a big opportunity," Ava said. "I don't quite know where to start. I've never really thought of myself as a fashion person. I'm more of a consumer than a creator."

"That's bloody nonsense," Sam said. "I've heard amazing things about you. But I think Nadine here has got the right idea. Use your own passions and inspirations to guide you. And lord knows your friend here has a style all her own," Sam said, jamming a thumb in Nadine's direction.

Nadine quickly glanced at Sam. He didn't look pissed off. Or disgusted. In fact, he was acting as though the barf episode had never happened. Nadine decided to take her cue from him.

"One of the things I notice about *Couture*," Nadine began falteringly, "is how slow the magazine's been to incorporate any kind of urban or hip-hop style. I mean it's everywhere in fashion, but totally missing from the magazine."

Sam nodded. God, he was scrumptious. "That's Isabel's Frenchness," he explained. "She doesn't get the whole hip-hop thing. Her context is very European."

Nadine continued. "I'm not saying we go all hoochie or anything, but I like the idea of mixing looks together. Like you, for instance," she said, appraising Sam's style. "You do the preppy-punk thing." Nadine stopped herself, suddenly embarrassed. What the hell was going on? Guys never had this effect on her. She wasn't acting like Nadine Van Buren, she-girl conqueror. She was acting more like Ava, the twenty-one-year-old virgin who'd never even had a boyfriend.

Sam smiled. "The preppy part comes from Eton, where I went to school on scholarship; the punk from East End London, where I grew up. And I agree that the juxtaposition of trends is the germ of fashion innovation."

Nadine felt her confidence growing. "So maybe we do something on hip-hop couture. There are probably lots of designers doing this kind of thing, beyond Kimora Lee Simmons. I bet we can even find hip-hop-influenced pieces from the fall collections and put them together. What do you think, Ava?"

Ava's eyes were bright with excitement. "I don't know much about hip-hop, but I do know that your idea sounds completely fresh."

"I agree," Sam said. "And I'll tell you what. If you two want to shoot a mock-up to illustrate your concept, I'll help. Nadine's a great photographer in her own right, but I can call in a friend to model for you. I've given a lot of girls their start, so I'm owed plenty of favors. I can also give you tips on how to style your concept because, trust me, no one understands Isabel's passions and pet peeves quite like I do," he said with a mock grimace.

Nadine couldn't believe how cool Sam was being. "You'd do that?" she asked.

"Of course, Nadine. I haven't forgotten that I promised to take you on that photo shoot in the country. I'll find something else for us to work on together, but while you have your hands full with this contest, I'm happy to lend you one of mine."

Nadine finally looked Sam in the eye. He was smiling again. Laugh lines crinkled around his eyes. If he thought she was an idiot, he was doing a damn fine job of covering it up. As Nadine was trying to think of a way to thank him, Ava did the honors and then Sam was off. Nadine's body was thrumming—with lust for Sam and excitement over hip-hop couture. She'd been relying on partying with Sly and naming the *Couture* spy to keep herself going over the last few weeks, but now her creative juices were starting to flow. She finally felt like she had something uniquely her own to offer the magazine. Maybe Kmart and Jimmy Choo were a hot combination after all.

3

Office Bitch

IT WAS FUNNY WHAT A difference a weekend and a few Google searches could make. Had Kiki announced that Aynsley was going to be working with Country Callie last Friday, well, let's just say that Aynsley would've rather committed to wearing an ABS knockoff dress to this Friday's VIP bash at the new club Key. But that was then. Now everything had changed.

And it was almost like Callie, the little faker, knew. Instead of hopping up and down with her usual annoying Midwestern gung-ho-ness, she was subdued. After the interns' meeting with Kiki, Callie had shuffled back to her desk, staring longingly at her best pal, Ava.

But Ava was working with Nadine now. She couldn't save Callie this time.

Callie looked at Aynsley with a note of panic in her hazel eyes. "Um, I just have to check my voice mail messages," she said nervously. Aynsley smirked. She wanted to savor this moment. She'd been waiting for it all summer.

"If you're expecting a call from Jules, he's in Vermont until tomorrow," Aynsley said casually. How it was that Aynsley's brother, Julian—dater of supermodels and European heiresses, hottest catch in all of Manhattan—was into this little pipsqueak of a liar was beyond her. Then again, Jules, though great for a party, wasn't exactly a paragon of depth. Maybe superficial attracted superficial.

Usually when Aynsley lorded her connection to Julian over Callie, the girl practically snarled, but now it was as if she didn't even notice. "I know he's out of town," she said hurriedly. "I'll just be a sec." She ran out of the room with her cell phone, looking as if she expected the sky to fall at any moment. How odd. Did she know Aynsley was onto her phony little act?

Callie returned five minutes later, wiping her palms against her white linen dress. "So, do you have any ideas? I have a couple, but they need to be developed."

"You'll want to get busy, then," Aynsley replied.

"You mean *we'll* want to get busy, right?" Callie stammered.

"Um, no," Aynsley said flatly. "Actually, you're going to come up with a fantastic idea and do the presentation, for the both of us."

Callie's pretty brow creased in confusion. "I don't understand. Did Kiki change her mind about the teams?"

"Nope. It's just that you'll be doing my work for me. Meaning you'll be doing the project for both of us."

Callie looked completely baffled. "Why would I do that?"

Aynsley's lips twitched into a slow, cruel grin. She was eating up Callie's discomfort like a chunk of Jacques Torres chocolate. "It's simple. You're my Office Bitch now."

Callie stared hard at Aynsley, her hazel eyes flashing with anger—*and fear*. "What are you talking about?"

Aynsley took a delicate sip from her Fiji water bottle and slowly replaced the cap before returning Callie's gaze. "What I mean," she said, "is that I'm onto you. I've caught you in a lie."

In response to Aynsley's words, Callie's practiced sophisticate-vixen look fell apart, and she instantly seemed like she was all of fourteen years old. Aynsley almost felt sorry for her. Almost.

"Wha—what do you mean?" Callie questioned her. "Did you talk to Quinn?"

"Who's Quinn?" Aynsley asked. How many lies had this girl told?

"Oh, no one. I just don't know what you're getting at. I mean— "

"Well, then, let me elucidate," Aynsley said, cutting Callie off before she'd managed to reveal even more. "I'm talking about Bexley Prep. 'One of the most exclusive schools in the Midwest,' I believe, is how you described it."

"Oh," said Callie, crestfallen.

Aynsley toyed with the diamonds on her Tiffany tennis bracelet. "I knew from the day we met that you were full of shit, Callie. It's just taken me this long to prove it."

"How'd you find out?" Callie croaked.

The truth of it was, Aynsley had found out because she herself had been found out. The morning after the gala she'd been awakened by an angry phone call from Gregory and Cecilia, her parents, who were currently summering in the world's most remote and dull Umbrian villa. Aynsley's parents knew that she hated the villa, with its appalling lack of trendy shops and hot guys. Which is why they were continually threatening to sequester her there all summer if she didn't get off her "indolent rear and show some initiative at *Couture*." After all, Cecilia had pulled major strings to secure Aynsley's internship.

Obviously, Cecilia Rothwell had no regard for the fact that her daughter had recently worked her tail off to pack *Couture*'s Cutting Edge Gala with all the right people. Lucy Gelson, the publicist who'd planned the gala, should have thanked Aynsley for getting such a splendid mix of celebs, trendsetters, and socialites to attend, making it one of the best shindigs this side of Marc Jacobs's Fashion Week after-party. But Lucy had instead tattled to Isabel that Aynsley had left her post at the velvet rope a little early, and Isabel—who'd been pals with Aynsley's mother since their college days at the Sorbonne—had immediately called Cecilia.

"You make one more stupid move," Cecilia had warned her in that diamond-hard, upper-crusty voice of hers, "and not only will you be stuck in Umbria for the summer, but you'll also have to take a job as a data-entry processor at your father's firm this fall." *Data entry?* Now, that was just cruel.

After Cecilia's transcontinental scolding, Aynsley had shuffled down the stairs of her family's Upper East Side town house and ambled into her mother's hideously decorated country kitchen in a dreadful mood. When Aynsley felt this bad, only two things made her feel better: a shopping spree, or a target upon which to aim her angst. So, with shopping out of the question at such an early hour, she set her sights on Callie.

Aynsley had spent the summer quietly investigating Callie, and she was more convinced than ever that the girl's luxe-life persona was about as real as one of those $15 Gucci knockoff bags sold down in Chinatown. All Aynsley needed was some concrete proof to her theory.

"Duh!" Aynsley had shouted to the empty kitchen. She'd been so busy feeding Callie enough rope to hang herself that she hadn't even bothered to do any online research—but it was time to vet Callie's cyber profile! Aynsley had run upstairs, turned on her PowerMac, and searched "Callie Ryan" using Dogpile.com. She'd found her, first at *Couture*'s Cutting Edge Showcase site, and then on MySpace. Callie's MySpace page had yielded few clues about Callie's hotshot school, Bexley Prep. So Aynsley quickly typed in Bexley School, Columbus, Ohio.

After a matter of minutes on the school's site, Aynsley realized exactly what was wrong. Bexley *wasn't* a prep school; it was just a regular public high school. Just to be sure she had it right, Aynsley IMed her cousin in Chicago to ask if she'd heard of this fancy private school in Columbus. And her cousin shot back a one-line response: *Exclusive prep school in Columbus? Are you serious?*

Of course, Aynsley didn't reveal her sources to Callie in the intern office that Monday morning. She just told her she'd figured out that her prep-school history was a big fat lie. "It would be one thing if you'd just fibbed to Ava, Nadine, and me," Aynsley said with a bitchy smirk. "But you put all this fake crap in your *Couture* bio?"

"But you wrote my bio!" Callie exclaimed. This was true. It was a stroke of luck for Aynsley when Kiki asked her to scribe bios for all the designers being honored at the Cutting Edge Gala. And when she interviewed Callie, she'd practically cornered the girl into fibbing.

"Yes, but I wrote it based on information that *you* provided," Aynsley said, all innocence. "I didn't think I'd need to fact-check. And I'm sure Isabel wouldn't be pleased to learn that you caused the magazine to publish a bunch of lies. I'm not sure how my brother would react, either. Julian hates a fake."

Callie, who was normally as puffed up as a Macy's Thanksgiving Day parade balloon, looked deflated and empty. "You're not going to tell on me, are you?" she asked pathetically.

Aynsley licked her lips and smiled. "Well, that depends on you. If you're a good office bitch and do as I say, then I'll keep quiet. But if you slack, I might just have to spill."

"I won't slack," Callie said miserably.

"Smart girl," Aynsley said, giving Callie a wicked wink. "Okay, then. We should stop our chitchatting. You've got work to do. There are only ten days between now and our presentation, and I expect to win this thing. It's quite important."

"But if it's so important, don't you think you should help me? I mean, we'll do a better job if we work together."

Aynsley shrugged. "You'll just have to work extra hard so it's *that* fantastic. And when I'm away from my desk, you make sure to tell people that I'm hard at work on our presentation. Understood?"

"Understood," Callie muttered, looking more defeated than angry.

"Excellent." Aynsley glanced at her BlackBerry. "Look at that. My friend Nikki wants to have lunch. I'm off. But I'll be back later this afternoon. Get cracking," she trilled.

Callie didn't respond. She just stared at her computer screen.

Aynsley pranced out of the office, utterly pleased with herself. This probably wasn't the kind of "initiative" her parents had in mind when they'd admonished her to up her game at *Couture*. But as far as Aynsley was concerned, it was ten times better.

4

Tabula Rasa

THERE WAS A WHOLE BIG world beyond her doorstep. Ava was just beginning to understand that. She emerged from an epic brainstorming meeting with Nadine, her head spinning with details about a whole subset of the fashion industry that was completely new to her. Sure, she'd been aware of some of the big hip-hop clothing lines: P. Diddy's Sean John, Jay-Z's Rocawear, and 50 Cent's G-Unit apparel. But in her mind, Ava had mistakenly reduced hip-hop fashion to baggy jeans, track suits, and bling.

Luckily, Nadine knew better, and thanks to her suggestion to juxtapose hip-hop and high fashion, they now had a concept: Bling Couture, a ten-page spread of photos, along with a cultural essay analyzing how street style was influencing casual wear as well as high-end design. They'd get someone brilliant like Malcolm Gladwell to write it, and the article would merge fashion spread and thinky trend piece. It was a new direction for *Couture*, and Ava thought the format would be groundbreaking. Or ground sinking—depending on Isabel's reaction. Then again, nothing ventured, nothing gained.

It was funny, but a year ago— —no, six weeks ago — Ava never would've had the guts to pitch such an ambitious piece. To be perfectly honest, she wouldn't have had the guts to pitch anything to *Couture*. But two weeks ago, she'd suggested a profile of Kain Ellis, a promising downtown designer. And now there was going to be an actual article about him in the magazine—with her byline.

Ava still couldn't believe it was all happening. She'd known she could write. She studied creative writing at Vassar. And she'd known she could do research; that was just a matter of finding the right trail and keeping on it. But even though she loved clothes and followed fashion, she'd always been the kind of girl who saw an outfit in the window of Club Monaco, bought it, and wore it as is. She'd never thought of herself as creative.

But something had happened the night of the Cutting Edge Gala. Ava wasn't sure exactly what it was, but she just knew that she was different. She was dying to rehash the proceedings with Callie. After all, it had been a huge night for her, too. Ava was also more than a little curious to hear how Callie and Aynsley— who on the best of days were as chummy as Angelina and Jen—were faring on their *Couture* collaboration.

She found Callie in the intern office, staring blankly at her computer screen, her skin as pale as her white linen dress.

"Hey," Ava called.

Callie jumped in her seat. "Oh, you scared me. Hi."

"Deep in fashion thought?"

"Something like that," Callie replied flatly.

"If you and Aynsley are done, I was thinking we could go across and get some cocktails at Poi. It's supposed to be amazing in there and they have like hundreds of varieties of sake. My treat," Ava offered.

"Sure," Callie replied, looking dazed. "I could use a drink."

Twenty minutes later, the pair made their way across Bryant Park to the cavernous three-story restaurant. Ava gasped at the cool interior, the backlit white lattice canopy, and swooping arches across the ceiling. At six the place was already mobbed. This was the watering hole of choice for Manhattan's publishing elite, which, come to think of it, made it a bit of a risky choice. But the new Ava wasn't scared of taking a few risks. At least, the right kind of risks. In fact, that was one of the things she'd been itching to talk to Callie about: She needed to confide in her about her whole sordid relationship with Daniel Aames—or *the Silver Fox*, as Nadine had christened him when she caught Ava with him a few weeks back. She wanted to tell Callie how she'd ended it, and that now she was free. Her life was a gloriously blank *tabula rasa*!

She and Callie sat down at a table next to the pond and ordered a bottle of Wakatake sake. After the waiter brought it out, along with two porcelain cups, Callie gulped down her glass in one go.

"Slow down, there," Ava said warmly. "I think you're supposed to sip it to savor the flavor."

Callie grabbed the bottle and poured herself another shot. "I'm not in a sipping mood."

Ava looked at her friend, who was staring gloomily into her glass. Normally, Callie would've been bouncing out of her seat in a place like this, crawling, as it was, with hot guys, fashionistas and, most important, powerful editors. Callie was one of the most loyal friends Ava had, but she was also the most ambitious person Ava had ever met, single-minded about her desire to become a famous designer. She'd done some seriously crazy things in the past few weeks, like plant her creations in *Couture*'s fashion closet. But the thing was, it had worked for her. She'd gotten her purses in the magazine, a major fashion coup.

"We haven't had a chance to talk much about the gala," Ava began. "Wasn't it just the most amazing night? I saw so many celebrities. J.Lo. Sienna Miller. Justin Timberlake was even there for, like, half a blink."

"Yeah, it was great," Callie replied absently.

"Soooo, what happened with you and Julian? He seemed all over you," Ava hinted.

Callie raised her perfectly square shoulders to her dainty ears. "Nothing much."

"Did you guys go out afterward?" Ava found it a little odd that Callie was being so coy. Usually, the girl was generous with details about her and Julian's escapades.

Callie shook her head. "He was going to Stowe the next day with some college friends, so we made it an early night."

The conversation hit a lull. "Did you catch the most recent Fashionista blog?" Ava asked, desperately trying to revive the evening. "Everyone's been talking about it."

"Yeah," Callie replied indifferently. "I've heard the buzz."

Out of things to say, Ava stared at the menu. Everything was exorbitant but she didn't care. She felt like celebrating. "Want to order some sushi? They're famous for it here."

When Callie declined, Ava knew something was wrong. The girl's appetite was endless, not that you'd guess it from her body: a perfectly toned five-foot-seven. Something must have happened with Aynsley. They'd probably argued during their ideas meeting. "Did you and Aynsley come up with any concepts?" Ava probed gently.

"One or two. How'd it go with Nadine?" Callie asked, looking like she couldn't care less how it went.

"Really good. I'm pretty excited about our project."

"That's great," Callie said, but she didn't try to pry any more information out of Ava. Again, this was weird. The Callie she knew would be craftily trying to size up the competition. But the Callie sitting across from her, absentmindedly playing with a dish of edamame, didn't seem to care at all. In a way, Ava was a bit relieved. She'd been worried about Callie seeing her as the competition. She knew how ruthless her friend could be and never expected her to be so blasé about the whole thing.

"You should come out to Port Jefferson with me next weekend," Ava suggested. "You can meet my parents. We can hit the beach. It's not the Hamptons, but it's still Long Island and it's really nice." Ava had been wanting to invite Callie out all summer, but, before, she couldn't. Her weekends had been reserved for secret meetings with Daniel, which were, thankfully, over.

"Okay, sure," Callie replied. "My tan is completely gone from being trapped in the office every day."

Encouraged by the fact that Callie had finally strung together an entire sentence, Ava pressed on. "I really wish you'd come out last weekend," she said. "It was so hot. And I was dying to talk to you about the gala. Something pretty major happened to me that night. . . ."

Callie's eyes registered the slightest flicker of interest. "Oh, yeah. Did you and Reese finally hook up?"

Reese Kimble was the adorable, funny, self-deprecating production assistant who Ava had met a few weeks back at a bar. Callie had been the one to introduce Ava to him, making good on her promise to find Ava a guy. At first she'd been mortified by Callie's obvious matchmaking, but Reese had made her laugh.

He seemed so sweet and so interested in her. And was *still* interested. He'd been emailing Ava for the last couple of weeks—funny anecdotes about the indie-actress diva whose movie he was working on, and goofy style questions that he said *proved* he needed Ava to do a fashion intervention for him, disguised as a date. Ava replied to his emails now and again, but—and Callie would kill her if she knew this—she'd thus far been noncommittal about going out with him. It wasn't that she didn't want to. It was just that, until gala night at least, her life had been too complicated.

"No, I didn't see Reese," Ava explained. "He wasn't at the gala. I mean, I don't think he could have gotten in."

Callie shrugged again. "All kinds of people got in. Aynsley was working the door, and she wasn't very selective."

"Did you and Aynsley have a fight or something?" Ava was accustomed to the rivalry between the two of them, but usually Callie gave as good as she got. She'd never seen her act this bitter and defeated.

A look of sadness flashed across Callie's face. "No. Everything's fine with Aynsley. Now, do you care if I order a Cosmo? This sake's giving me a headache."

"Order whatever you want," Ava offered. "But are you sure you're okay?"

"Back off!" Callie snapped, instantly looking shocked at the force of her own reprimand. Then her full lips started to tremble. "I'm sorry, Ava."

"Cal, what is it? What's wrong?"

"Everything's ruined, that's what," Callie moaned.

"What are you talking about? You're on top of the world."

"Ha! Well, if I am, I'm about to fall far and hard." The dam broke and Callie's tears came fast and furious.

Ava reached over. "Tell me what's going on," she said, gently touching her friend's hand.

And so Callie did. In a long, meandering, emotional monologue, Callie explained everything: A few weeks ago she'd gone on her first date with Julian to the Brooklyn neighborhood of Williamsburg. While cruising the art galleries, she happened upon a hat designer who was selling some silk screens. Callie had bought the material and then spent the entire week feverishly sewing the silk screens into purses—the very purses that had landed her in the Cutting Edge Designers Showcase.

"I never planned to pass off the silk screens as my own," Callie said, awash in fresh tears. "Isabel and Marceline just assumed they were mine and I was so overwhelmed at the prospect of getting my stuff in the magazine that I just let them think it. I was gonna square it with Quinn, the silk-screen designer, but everything happened so fast and he saw the article and confronted me at the gala. Now he and I have to meet with Marceline and explain the whole thing, and I'm just done for. I know it."

"Let me get this straight," Ava said. "The fabric was someone else's but you designed the bags?"

"Right." Callie sniffed.

"This guy Quinn didn't help you design the bags?"

"No. I bought the fabric from him and never saw him again—until the night of the gala."

"Well, it's not great that you misled the staffers about the fabric, but I think the important thing is that *you* created the bags. Designers don't normally weave their own fabric. They buy it from other people. What matters is that the vision for the bags came from you. So—I don't think this is the end of the world, Cal."

"How can you say that?" Callie asked miserably. "I've been living a lie. I've made a mockery of a hallowed fashion institution. I'm a total fake. In fashion, there's no worse sin."

Callie gulped down her Cosmo and took a deep breath. She dried her eyes with a cocktail napkin and stared at Ava. "I'm sorry to unload all this on you. And here you obviously wanted to tell me something. So what's the major thing that happened to you at the gala?"

Ten minutes ago, Ava, practically floating with a newfound sense of freedom, had been eager to tell Callie her secret. Ava had assumed that Callie of all people would understand what Ava had done and why—Callie, who like Ava felt like an outsider in the glamorous world of high fashion. Callie, who like Ava wanted to be on the inside, the way Aynsley was. But now Ava wasn't so sure. If Callie judged herself this harshly for passing off someone's fabric as her own, what would she think of Ava's scandalous transgressions?

"Oh, it was nothing," Ava said. "I met Karl Lagerfeld, is all."

She hadn't really, but what was one more lie on top of so many others?

"Enemies are so stimulating." –Katharine Hepburn

Filed under: Fashionista > Style

My loyal readers have most likely discerned by now that there are a few things the Fashionista simply cannot abide: 1) Designer knockoffs. 2) Social climbers 3) Liars, and 4) People who are bitchy for sport. But the Fashionista would be one of the before-mentioned Liars, were I not to admit that I do enjoy a good catfight now and then. Better yet? A good rivalry.

Indeed, rivalries have sparked more than a few hot romances—if you doubt me, give Shakespeare's *The Taming of the Shrew* a read. Animosity makes for fabulous tabloid fodder— *Paris* vs. *Nicole*. Paris vs. *Lindsay*. Paris vs. . . . And, more important, discord has inspired some of the greatest fashion innovation of our time, » and I'm not simply talking about Jeffrey vs. Angela, _Project Runway_: Season III.

Take that notorious fashion feud between two Czech models (I _know_ you know who I mean)—both gorgeous, both successful—which culminated in one of them chopping off her hair, so as not to be mistaken for her archrival. Her vengeful coif became the most copied haircut this side of the Katie Holmes bob. And let us not forget the notorious rivalry between _Couture_ magazine's Isabel Dupre and the aging punk designstress, Alexandra Foxwood. Their mutual disdain has fired their desire to outdo each other for years, and the fashion world can do nothing but thank them for refusing to forgive and forget.

The obvious trick to making the most of one's rivalries is to maintain one's dignity. Case in point: That bratty Brooklyn designer who hired goons to smash her competitor's shop windows is now too mired in legal fees to stock her own shop. So take Isabel and Alexandra's lead—compete until you're the last woman standing, but do it on the up-and-up and, of course . . . never let your enemy catch you underdressed.

Your faithful Fashionista

5

Strip Poker—Minus the Poker

CALLIE WONDERED HOW it was humanly possible to hate one Rothwell as much as she lusted after the other one.

Aynsley had made Callie's work life a living hell. In addition to covering the lazy cow's usual *Couture* duties, like answering emails and helping the fashion department messenger boxes of clothes to designers, Aynsley had forced Callie to conjure up countless excuses for the socialite's prolonged absences from the magazine. (As far as the editorial staff knew, Aynsley was out doing research for their project, but Callie knew that the only thing Aynsley was researching was next fall's suede stiletto boots at Barneys.) On top of that, Callie had her own daily responsibilities to complete: going through the slush pile of unsolicited manuscripts and answering *Couture*'s general email account. Oh, right, and in her "spare" time, she was supposed to be dreaming up a fantastic concept for a new fashion feature.

Normally, the opportunity to strut her stuff for the *Couture* staff would've had Callie dancing down 42nd Street. And weirdly enough, when Kiki had told her she'd be working with Aynsley, she'd actually been dumb enough to think that with Aynsley's high-fashion smarts and Callie's do-it-yourself know-how, the two of them would be a dream team. Ha!

It didn't matter one way or the other now. Callie was too tapped out to come up with an even remotely interesting concept for a ten-page fashion feature. Every time she took out her sketch pad, she got caught up in alternately seething at Aynsley and obsessing about her looming showdown with Quinn. When she'd impulsively confessed her secret about the purses to Ava, she'd hoped it would make her feel better, but all it had really done was confirm that the entire mess was real. Of course Ava had been nice about it. But Ava was nice about everything. And Callie couldn't bear telling her the rest of the story, about her fake prep school past and Aynsley's office blackmail.

"Hello, Callie. Anyone call for me while I was away?" Aynsley was standing in the entrance to the intern office, glowing from a Bliss facial and a shopping spree—which had netted her the white Catherine Malandrino shirt-dress and the Tod's feather-embellished Dee ballerina flats she was currently wearing.

"Kiki and Nadine were looking for you," Callie reported. "I told Kiki you were hunting for fabrics in Chinatown. And I told Nadine you were shopping in Nolita," Callie said, unable to hide her disdain.

"I asked you to alert me if any senior staffers called me. I didn't see any emails," Aynsley said, waving her BlackBerry Pearl.

Callie suppressed the urge to hurl a Rolodex at Aynsley's smirking face. "Kiki just called five minutes ago. And I've been buried with your *other* work," Callie snarled.

"That's nice," Aynsley said with a laugh. She eyed Callie with her laser-beam gaze, obviously taking in Callie's outfit, the one thing Callie felt good about today. She was wearing a skin-tight blue-gray pencil skirt that she'd sewn herself, a sleeveless white Emporio Armani tuxedo top that she'd borrowed from Ava, and a skinny tie and black leather armband that she'd picked up at Trash & Vaudeville. Fishnets and Kenneth Cole Reaction patent-leather high-heeled Mary Janes completed the look—all part of her new "office bitch" style, which was the one good thing to come from being Aynsley's slave. "Well, aren't you gussied up," Aynsley intoned. "What's the occasion?"

"A date," Callie bragged. The only thing she still held over Aynsley these days was Julian Rothwell. He was as interested in Callie as ever. In fact, tonight he was taking her out somewhere special. He'd promised.

A look of distaste crossed Aynsley's pretty face, giving Callie a sliver of satisfaction.

"Ah, Jules. What's tonight's offbeat locale?" Aynsley asked. "Some arty Brooklyn nabe? A picnic? Dinner at some grungy restaurant only he knows about? My brother loves to prove his hipster cred when he's out with new girls."

Callie's moment of contentment quickly passed. Those had indeed been the type of dates Julian had taken her on. Had he told Aynsley the details? And *new girls*? What the hell did that mean? Callie was used to Aynsley taking every opportunity she could to imply that Callie was nobody special, so she tried to keep her look as impassive as possible. Which only made Aynsley laugh.

"I'm going to check in with Kiki and then I'm out of here," she said. "Do call Nadine for me and tell her to meet me at Chow Bar at eight."

"I'm not your secretary," Callie fumed.

Aynsley stared her down. "No, but you *are* my office bitch. And that means you do what I say. *Got it?* Good."

By the time seven rolled around, Callie was in dire need of a cocktail. As usual, Julian was being coy about their plans for the evening. He'd told Callie to meet him outside the Time Warner Center at Columbus Circle at eight. So Callie sat in the empty office fidgeting until seven forty-five. She wished that Ava or even Nadine was around so they could grab a drink with her before her date. She was furious with Aynsley for casting a cloud over her night with Julian—the one bright spot in an otherwise hideous week—and she needed something to take the edge off.

But when she spotted Julian standing in the distance, tan and seductive in a cream-colored linen suit paired with beat-up Prada suede sandals, Callie felt much of the week's weight lift from her. There was something about watching him wait for her that was unbelievably sexy. And then there was Julian himself: tall with black curly hair, green-blue eyes, and an ever-amused look on his face, as if he were thinking something slightly lascivious but was too much of a gentleman to admit it. Callie admired the view for a moment before sneaking up behind him and putting her hands over his eyes.

Without looking, Julian placed his hands on Callie's hips, spun her around, and kissed her, long and slow. *Now that's more like it*, Callie thought.

"How'd you know it was me?" Callie asked when they came up for air. "What if you'd just kissed some low-rent bridge-and-tunnel chick?"

Julian laughed. "You're such a snob! I recognized you by your sexy scent," he said, nibbling on her neck. "And even if it hadn't been you, I figured only a hot chick would wear that perfume."

"Julian!" Callie exclaimed, smacking him on the arm with her black leather portfolio. "You're a bad, bad boy."

"You don't know the half of it," he leered. "And ouch. Your briefcase packs quite a punch."

"It's not my briefcase. It's my portfolio. I keep leaving it at *Couture*. Don't let me forget it tonight."

"You have any sexy pictures in there?"

"Like girls without dresses? No, just dresses without girls. So what's on tonight's agenda? The outer boroughs? Queens? Maybe Staten Island?"

Julian's grin was as smooth as melting chocolate. "None of the above," he said. "Puerto Rico."

"Huh?" Callie's heart started racing. Obviously, Julian was planning to jet her off to some gorgeous beach in Puerto Rico the way Richard Gere took Julia Roberts to San Francisco in *Pretty Woman*. She'd never even been to Puerto Rico—not that she'd admit that. But flying there on a private jet for one night? Now *that* was the kind of date she'd always dreamed a New York prince like Julian would have up his sleeve.

"Well, not Puerto Rico exactly," Julian said, ruining Callie's fantasy. "I'm taking you salsa dancing at Lincoln Center," he explained.

Callie tried to hide her disappointment. "*Salsa dancing?* Isn't that kind of . . . urban?"

"God, you're worse than Aynsley," Julian said with a devilish grin. "Trust me, dancing at Lincoln Center can be a pretty star-studded affair. Last time I spotted Maggie Gyllenhaall and Peter Sarsgaard spinning around. Conan O'Brien shows sometimes, too."

Well, that sounds a little more promising, Callie thought. "But I don't know how to salsa," she admitted.

"Don't worry. I'll teach you," he assured her. "It's so beautiful out tonight. It'll be perfect." Julian took her hand and began leading her up Amsterdam Avenue.

When they got to Lincoln Center, she had to admit that it did look pretty magical. There was a big square set up for dancing by the circular fountain in the central plaza. Fairy lights were strung over the dance floor, and all around them glamorous people dressed for the theater made their way inside. Callie could see the giant Chagall murals through the large windows of the Metropolitan Opera House. She was a little like Julia Roberts, after all—Richard Gere took her to the opera in *Pretty Woman*, too.

"Drink?" Julian asked. "Salsa calls for rum, don't you think?"

"Sure, whatever you're having," Callie replied.

Julian returned with two fruity drinks that went down like candy. It was only after Callie had finished her second that she realized why the drink was called *punch*. By her third cocktail, she was feeling no pain. One awful work week was behind her and the uncertainty of the one before her felt miles away.

"Wooh, this is so much fun," she said as Julian expertly twirled her around. "Is this step the *paso abierto*?"

"That's when you twirl out. In is *paso finto*," Julian replied.

"Where'd you learn to salsa like this?"

"J.Lo taught me," he replied casually.

Callie stopped midturn. "She did not! You're teasing me."

Julian raised his eyebrows noncommittally and pulled Callie back toward him. God, had Callie known that salsa was this sexy, she would've learned how to do it years ago. It was like she and Julian were totally fooling around, much more than they had on any of their previous dates. Except tonight it was all out in the open, with fifty other couples doing the exact same thing.

Julian seemed to be feeling the same way because after an hour or so of sweaty hip grinding, he leaned in and whispered in her ear. "I'm afraid if we stay on this dance floor any longer, things are going to get X-rated."

Callie giggled coyly. "We wouldn't want to be arrested for indecency. Imagine the scandal if we got our names in the papers."

"No. Certainly not," Julian said with mock seriousness. "I had planned on taking you to dinner at Masa, but the only thing I want to devour right now is you."

Callie had been waiting for Julian to take her somewhere fancy like Masa, but now, her lust outweighed her desire to eat at New York's trendiest eateries. "That's okay. I've been to Masa before," she lied. "And

I don't have much of an appetite at the moment . . . for food, anyhow."

Julian grinned wolfishly. "I think it's time you saw Chez Rothwell."

Callie froze. Chez Rothwell was home to the last person she wanted to see: Aynsley! Julian seemed to read her mind. "Don't worry. Sly doesn't come home on Friday nights until the wee hours of Saturday morning. And my bedroom's on an entirely different floor from hers. No awkward encounters, I promise."

"Why would I be worried about Sly?" Callie asked. Of course, there were plenty of reasons, but she wasn't about to get into that. In fact, she was actually dying to see the Rothwell town house. Nadine had been gushing about it for weeks, and Callie was going to love sharing every detail about the Upper East Side mansion with her friends back in Ohio.

"Let's walk across the park. It'll be quicker than getting a taxi," Julian said. He grabbed her hand and pulled her toward Central Park, spinning her around the paths, trying out some of their salsa moves, and then pulling her behind a tree to nibble on her neck. The next thing Callie knew they were standing before a grand three-story brownstone with an actual lantern burning in the front yard. It was the kind of place Callie had only seen in movies. She couldn't believe Julian and Aynsley actually lived here.

Julian led her up the steps and into the foyer where Callie came face-to-face with a painting that looked like—*could it be an original Monet?*

"Mother's pride and joy," Julian affirmed. "She loves anything floral and formal, as you can see." He shook his head and sighed. "Even though she's five thousand miles away, you can feel her oppressive taste."

"It's amazing," Callie swooned. "We don't have Monets at our place." Callie wracked her brain to think of a comparable work of art. "We have a Matisse," she exclaimed. It wasn't entirely untrue. There was a Matisse *print* in the kitchen.

"Ah, Father has a small Matisse in his office," Julian replied. "Personally, I think the Monet's prettier, but it makes this house feel even more like a museum. Actually, what this place needs is a good mussing up." He leaned in and unknotted the tie around Callie's neck, depositing it on the landing before the staircase. "Much better," he said.

"My turn," Callie said, as she slid Julian's linen jacket onto the first step.

"Hmm," Julian replied, kissing Callie's neck and moving up a stair. "Quid pro quo." He snaked his arm down the front of Callie's shirt, down her skin-tight skirt, to her calves and undid each of her shoes.

"This is fun. It's like strip poker—minus the poker." Callie giggled and then felt a jolt of excitement as Julian's hands enveloped her waist and peeled away her fishnets.

"No fair. You have more parts to your outfit," Julian murmured. "I'll be naked first."

"Poor baby," Callie said, running her hands along his perfectly cut chest before undoing the button on his pants.

They went one for one all the way up to Julian's bedroom on the second floor. And wouldn't you know it, by the time they reached his door, neither of them was wearing any clothes?

"Game over," Julian said, opening the door to his bedroom. But Callie had a feeling that the game had just begun.

6

Charity Case

AYNSLEY WAS ANNOYED EVEN before she walked in the front door. Her night out had been a total bust. She'd planned to meet Nadine at Chow Bar for a light dinner after which they were going to take advantage of Aynsley's VIP invitation to opening night at Key—a club that was so exclusive it didn't have a marked door or a phone number (not a listed one, anyway). To get in, you had to be invited. It was all very top-secret, and Aynsley had made several phone calls to get on the list. She'd secured spots for herself, Nadine, and her Dalton friends Hayden and Spencer. She'd been looking forward to playing with the crème of the party set: Britney,

Paris, Lindsay—depending on who was in rehab this week.

Nadine had shown up for their eight o'clock dinner at nine ten. Naturally, Aynsley had been late herself, but only a half hour, which was fine. Everyone knew that up to forty-five minutes tardy was still in good taste. Anything beyond that was both lame and inconsiderate.

When Nadine finally strolled in, Aynsley's annoyance was mixed with suspicion. Nadine wasn't wearing any of her usual neon-lit, cleavage-boosting, thigh-skimming apparel. No foot-long earrings or mile-high platforms. Not even a wig, weave, fall, or scarf. Just a pair of Diesel jeans and a gauzy sequined DKNY tank top. And, most telling, she was wearing flats! Nadine, on the south side of five foot two, was endlessly trying to correct her height deficit with dizzyingly high footwear.

"Didn't you have time to change after work?" Aynsley asked Nadine when she walked in.

"No, I changed," Nadine had replied. "I'm just feeling a mellow vibe tonight."

Then, as they ordered dinner, things only got worse. Nadine couldn't stop blathering about the *Couture* project she was putting together with Ava. But she remained annoyingly mum about the details of said project. Not that Aynsley cared. If she gave two shits about winning, she would never have let fashion-deficient Country Callie take control. (Okay, Callie's aesthetic had improved hugely since she'd arrived in New York, but the girl had miles to go.) Then, over their salad course, Nadine casually mentioned that she was planning on buckling down and getting serious—so serious that she might go home after dinner and forgo their big night at Key.

Aynsley had fought too hard to get Nadine's name on the list to just let her friend go home early. So, in the end, she'd been forced to cajole Nadine—the biggest party whore she'd ever met—into coming to Key.

That whole episode had been aggravating enough. But then, after leaving Chow Bar, they'd met Spencer and Hayden at Casa SoHo for drinks, and a drunk tourist spilled sangria all over Aynsley's new dress.

When they arrived at Key, things got even worse. Aynsley's name wasn't even on the list. Beyond humiliating. Worse still, she had to resort to calling Walker Graystone—the irritating hipster party promoter and video director who was endlessly pestering Aynsley to go out with him—to get her in. Because she'd stooped to calling Walker, Aynsley had to agree to go out for a drink with him. And by the time her name had magically reappeared on the list and the bitchy door wench had let her into the club, Aynsley was beyond fed up.

"This place was over before it even started," she'd proclaimed to Nadine, Spencer, and Hayden.

"You're kidding, right?" Hayden asked, gesturing to the bloodred banquettes, baroque candelabras, and surfeit of bored-looking models. "Look at all the babes. This place is smokin'."

"Whatever" was Aynsley's retort. "I'm out of here."

"You can't go now. You went through all that hassle to get us in," Nadine exclaimed.

"So my job is done," Aynsley said with a haughty flip of her hair. And, before anyone had a chance to object, she was out the door and hailing a cab uptown.

On her way home, Aynsley had planned to spend the rest of the evening in her Vera Wang PJs, sipping Pinot Grigio, while going through her back issues of *Women's Wear Daily*. But when she walked through her front door, she was greeted by a trail of clothes on the stairs. Her first thought was *The house has been robbed*! But then she saw the skinny tie. The portfolio. The fishnets. And a linen suit that was obviously Julian's because it bore the little label of the Hong Kong tailor who'd made it for him.

Aynsley trod up the stairs, picking up items of clothing as she went, her anger building with each new acquisition. By the time she reached Jules's bedroom door, she was ready to explode.

"Sly, is that you?" Julian called from inside.

"No, it's the maid," Aynsley sneered as she threw open the door and flung the clothes on the floor. She didn't think she could be any angrier, but when she looked up, she was beyond furious. There was Julian, lounging in that ridiculous mahogany bed of his. On his face, he wore a conspiratorial grin, as if he'd just told Aynsley the punchline to an inside joke. And there, next to Aynsley's smug-looking brother, was a terrified-looking Callie, pulling Cecilia's 600-thread-count Egyptian sheets up around her slightly freckled shoulders. Her mane of dirty-blond hair was perfectly tousled, and Aynsley couldn't help but notice that it was the kind of bedhead you could only get from actually rolling around in bed.

"Three's company," Julian said. "Care for a glass of wine?"

"Excuse me. Are you suggesting that I'm the company? Because last I checked I lived here. As for your little friend," she said, her voice dripping with disgust, "she's a little bit *out* of your company."

"You're talking in riddles, Sly. Just say what you mean," Julian insisted.

Aynsley felt her anger threatening to boil over, but she summoned her cool and icy side over her fury. "What I *mean* is, what the hell are you doing dating Callie, Julian? Have you lost your mind?"

Julian shrugged. Aynsley wanted to smack the imperious look off his face.

"Honestly, Jules. This is so against type for you," she said bitchily. "Last time I checked, Callie wasn't an heiress. Or a model. The Ryans of Columbus, Ohio, don't own any power companies or department stores. So, seriously, what exactly are you doing with Callie? Is she in your little black book under Charity Case?"

Julian's lazy eyes glazed over with amusement. Callie, on the other hand, looked like she was about to throw up. She was staring at Aynsley, her expression both beseeching and murderous as if begging her enemy not to give her up, while at the same time wanting to throttle her for having the power to do it.

Julian finally looked at Callie. "Sorry. I thought we'd have the place to ourselves tonight."

"Um. Right. I should go," Callie stammered. She slid out of bed with the sheet clutched around her as she slinked toward the door.

"Don't forget these," Aynsley said, kicking the sad little heap of clothing she'd collected toward a mortified Callie. Holding the sheet in one hand, Callie rifled through the pile, finding her skirt, shirt, and shoes and abandoning the rest. Then, shooting Aynsley one more meaningful glance, she backed out of the door and was gone.

"Well, that was a fun little drama," Julian said, sliding out of bed and stepping into a pair of boxers. Aynsley looked away. Obviously, her brother thought every female in the world wanted to see his naked ass. She was *his sister*, for god's sake.

"Can you hand me my linen trousers?" he said. Aynsley flung the suit pants his way, willing herself to calm down. Her brother wasn't making it easy.

"Really, Sly. You didn't have to treat the girl so shabbily."

"*I* didn't have to treat her shabbily?"

"Well, yes. A little discretion wouldn't have been the worst thing in the world. Lord knows I've looked the other way when you've entertained guys in your boudoir."

"I can't believe you just called it a boudoir. You're such a goddamn cliché."

"There you go, speaking in riddles again."

"Can you even name one friend of mine who you haven't hooked up with?" Aynsley asked.

"I didn't hook up with Nadine," Julian said with a touch of pride. "And I had ample opportunity."

"Please. The only reason you didn't jump Nadine the night of our last party was because Chiara was here and you'd already hooked up with her. But for chrissakes, Julian, you've slept with so many of my friends. It's getting so I'm hesitant to bring anyone around these days. You're like the horny old family dog, humping the leg of every pretty girl I know."

For a second, Julian looked insulted. But then he just laughed. Aynsley wanted to slug him. "Well, no one else has complained," he said. "And besides, I didn't think you and Callie were friends, anyhow. She seems to loathe the sight of you."

Julian had obviously thought this would piss Aynsley off, but it had the opposite effect. It cooled her down. "That is entirely beside the point," she retorted. "*The point* is that you're a slut. You've screwed every girl in the 10021 zip code, plus half the European socialite set. You're like a slutty social climber. Which is perplexing, because you're *already* on top. Why climb?"

"Well, now you're just contradicting yourself," Julian said, his eyes looking arrogant and bored. "If you think I'm such an heiress stalker, then you should be proud that I'm sharing the wealth with a little Midwestern rube."

"Midwestern rube!" Aynsley fumed. "How dare you?"

"Simmer down, will you, Sly? You're making a huge deal over a little fling. Callie and I were just having some fun. You know, *Do a little dance, make a little love*," he said mimicking an old disco anthem.

"Does Callie know that's all you've been doing?" Aynsley asked.

"I would think so. I haven't given her reason to suspect anything else. Good god, we've been on, like, one and a half dates. Hardly what I'd call a major courtship."

Suddenly, Aynsley was all out of fight. The truth was, she'd seen her brother work a thousand girls in the same exact way. Usually, her attitude was *caveat emptor*—buyer beware. And most girls could suss out what kind of guy her charming brother really was. Callie, however, was different. Somehow, Aynsley could tell that she thought Julian genuinely cared about her, and when Callie finally found out what a sleazebag Julian really was, Aynsley was pretty sure that the girl was going to be crushed.

The thing Aynsley couldn't figure out was, *Why did she care?*

7

Breakfast at Tiffany's, Cocktails at Bergdorf's

A DATE. AVA HAD A DATE. Not some secret rendezvous, but a coffee date, in the Village, with Reese. Just like that.

Yesterday, he'd sent her another one of the casual, quirky emails that he'd been sending her for weeks. Ava didn't know much about nice guys, but she felt like Reese deserved a girl who didn't have a lot of baggage—so she'd held off on accepting a date with him until her baggage got a little less complicated.

Now, with Daniel Aames out of her life, Ava was feeling a lot more worthy of Reese. Things were going so well at *Couture*, and she wasn't about to let the mistakes she'd made with Daniel define her. It was time to get her personal life on track.

Reese had emailed her a breezy little note about the busy life of a high-powered fashionista—and suggested they meet for coffee: "If and when you have the time," he wrote. "You can think of it as multitasking; the caffeine will keep you up and working longer, so by having coffee with me, you'll be doing yourself and the whole fashion world a generous favor."

Ava had laughed out loud at his missive. And then she accepted his invitation before she had the chance to chicken out.

This morning, she'd woken up ridiculously giddy with excitement, and it took her forever to decide what to wear. In the end, she chose an outfit that the old Ava would have found a little daring: a green rayon vintage forties dress with big crystal buttons, paired with a funky gray frayed blazer that Callie designed, and the pair of pewter Manolos that Callie had worn to the Cutting Edge Gala. Ava piled her dark brown hair into a retro-looking bun, and instead of her usual Prada nude lip gloss, she painted her sweetheart lips with Chanel Barcelona Red.

Usually when she experimented with a new look, she felt silly, like she was playing dress-up. But when she'd given herself a final once-over in the mirror this morning, she just knew—*she looked pretty damn good*.

When she got to the office, Nadine whistled. "Well, aren't you the vintage diva today," she said with a grin.

"I have a date!" Ava blurted, unable to contain herself. She'd wanted to tell Callie first, but Callie had been so glum, and preoccupied with her project, that Ava hadn't had the chance.

"Oh, yeah? Second date with the Silver Fox?" Nadine teased. Thankfully, she added, "Just kidding," before Ava had a chance to object.

"I told you—I was interviewing *the Silver—I mean*—that older designer. His name is Kain Ellis, by the way," Ava fibbed. "Anyhow, my date is nothing major, just coffee." She could feel herself grinning like the world's biggest goofball.

"Coffee can turn into dinner, and dinner turns into a whole lot of things," Nadine said with an impish wink. She sure was peppy this morning—in mood, anyway. Her clothes, usually a degree of risqué that Ava could only dream of pulling off, were totally understated. She had on a knee-length khaki BCBG cargo skirt, a white fitted Gap tank, and a pair of Converse low-tops. Her camera hung from her neck.

"Are you going on a shoot or something?" Ava asked.

"As a matter of fact, I am," Nadine said, beaming. "Didn't you get my voice mail?"

"Uh, no," Ava said, glancing at her phone and seeing that she had a message.

"We're kicking our Bling Couture idea into high gear. Sam's taking me to the Bronx so we can get some shots of street style on the actual streets. While we cover that end, I need you to case the high-fashion world. Hit the three Bs: Barneys, Bendel's, Bergdorf's, and take note of anything that fits our whole luxury street-style concept. Tomorrow we'll shoot a few samples on a model and then present the whole package to Kiki and Isabel. Hopefully Isabel will be in a good mood. I heard she wasn't all that pleased to be mentioned on *Fashionista* with Alexandra Foxwood, but then again, it's good PR for *Couture*. Either way, I bet we knock her socks off!"

Ava had never seen Nadine so excited—although she couldn't be entirely sure if it was their project or Sam that had her buzzing. In any event, Ava's day was only getting better. An assignment to spend the day shopping! Followed by a coffee and who-knows-what-else with Reese? Perfection!

"Sounds like a plan," Ava said. "Should I just take notes?"

"Well, if you can be sneaky about it, get some snaps, too," Nadine said, handing her a Canon Elph. "And if you see something that's just slam-bang perfect, buy it. We can shoot it and return it tomorrow—or *expense it* if our story's chosen. But let's steer clear of the sample closet for now. Don't want the spy, or Callie or Aynsley for that matter, to know what we're up to. By the way, don't say a word to Callie. I haven't mentioned any details to Sly, which I think is killing her—but hey, business is business."

Sam Owens popped his head into the intern office. "Good morning, ladies. Nadine, I've got to nip over to the lab to look at some proofs now, but I should be ready to take off in about an hour."

"Cool," Nadine said casually.

"You want anything? Need any film? Or a coffee? I was going to grab an iced Americano before we head out."

Ava watched as Nadine's face took on a rosy blush. "I'll take an iced triple cappuccino," she said shyly.

Sam raised his eyebrows. "Triple, eh? Girl likes to live on the edge."

Ava kept her eyes on Nadine as she watched Sam leave. She could practically feel the sparks. "He's so nice," Ava offered.

"I know," Nadine replied. "I still can't figure out what his game is."

"Does everyone have to have a game?" Ava asked.

Nadine shot Ava her best *are-you-for-real?* look. "Honey, everyone's got game. Some people just don't know that they're playin'."

After lunch, Ava set out on her shopping expedition, and before she knew it, she'd spent four hours taking photos of all sorts of goodies. She'd seen Versace red dresses, their plunging necklines secured by ruby-encrusted dollar-sign brooches, leopard-print Vivienne Westwood bias-cut gowns, an Alice Roi halter top and matching low-slung skirt adorned with a metal belt, $225 silk dewrags, $700 neon-orange track suits, and $1,200 hoodie dresses. Earlier in the week, she and Nadine had pored over old issues of *Vibe*, with Nadine pointing out styles that had filtered from the hip-hop world on up. It amazed Ava that once she knew what to look for, she saw the street-style influence on couture everywhere.

Ava glanced at her Tag Heuer watch. It was almost five o'clock, and she was due to meet Reese in an hour. As she left Bergdorf's, she spotted something shiny out of the corner of her eye and went over to investigate. It was a suit, with a silver lamé fitted jacket and matching hot pants. The cut of the jacket was old-school, but the silver fabric and revealing pants were totally street. It was the perfect juxtaposition. After making sure that the suit was returnable, she charged all $895 of it on her Visa. Then she walked out of Bergdorf's on a high, as if she'd just bought this gorgeously outrageous outfit for herself. In a strange way, maybe she had.

Bergdorf's windows were Ava's favorite among all of the Manhattan department stores and she lingered, enjoying every detail. It was the end of July, so the displays were still full of brightly colored frocks, knee-length shorts paired with dizzying pumps, peep-toe shoes, and straw handbags. But in a week, the storefront would switch to fall offerings: tweedy jackets, cashmere sweaters, sexy trench coats. It was a happy reminder that—even though the mercury was in the nineties—crisp autumn days were just around the corner.

"Well, well, well, aren't you a vision? Breakfast at Tiffany's, cocktails at Bergdorf's, perhaps? A modern-day Audrey Hepburn."

Ava swung around to find Daniel Aames in all his silver foxiness staring back at her. Even in a city of eight million people, she'd managed to bump into the one person she most wanted to avoid. *Daniel*—perfectly composed in a gray pin-striped suit and Armani sunglasses—didn't look the least bit surprised to see her.

"Hello," Ava said, extending her cheek forward to be kissed. She knew Daniel would expect civility, even though their last meeting had been anything *but* civil. "What are you doing here?" she asked politely.

"A little shopping for my wife," he explained. "Birthday's coming up next week."

Ava had seen Daniel's wife, a pretty woman with jet-black hair, on a few occasions, but they'd never met. "Oh, tell her happy birthday for me," she said lamely.

They stood there casually and Ava hoped this exchange of pleasantries would be the extent of it. After all, she'd made her feelings perfectly clear at the Cutting Edge Gala when she told Daniel that their little arrangement had to end.

"Do you have time for a quick drink?" Daniel asked. "I don't really care for the way we left things."

"Um, I don't, actually," Ava confessed. "I'm—I'm meeting someone."

Daniel smiled. "Well then, we'll just have to chat here."

Ava desperately wanted to leave, to be as tough and resolute as she'd been at the gala. But Daniel hadn't gotten as far as he had without charisma. Like it or not, he had a strange hold on her. So instead of telling him she had to leave and flouncing off like that other Hepburn—Katharine—might have, she just said "Okay."

"That was quite a party last week. *Couture* certainly knows how to throw an event," Daniel offered.

"Uh, yeah, it was nice," Ava replied, keeping up her end of the chit-chat.

"And that was some mention you got in the Fashionista blog. Transformed from mousy girl to fashion Cinderella—you've certainly come a long way, Ava."

Ava shrugged. She was still baffled—and flattered—that the Fashionista had singled her out, but she wasn't about to discuss that with Daniel.

"Maybe that's why you've changed your mind about me. Now that you're an It Girl, you don't feel our relationship is necessary anymore, is that right?"

"That's not why," Ava replied. "And I'm no It Girl."

"Well then, I don't quite know what prompted your sudden change of heart, but I don't think you can expect to break things off unilaterally," Daniel said firmly.

"How else would I do it? Am I supposed to ask your permission?" Ava mused.

Something in Daniel's smile shifted then, as an edginess shadowed his face. "It's not really as simple as that. There's a lot at stake."

"Exactly," Ava cried. "A whole lot at stake for *me*. Do you expect me to throw away a chance at happiness and success because of you?"

"Ahh, so you think happiness and success are waiting for you elsewhere? Sweet Ava has found greener pastures."

Ava didn't know what else to offer but the truth. "Yes. And because what we were doing was wrong. You must know that!"

Daniel laughed again. The sound was hard and metallic. "You can't really be that naïve. To think that you're trading deception for truth and happiness."

"Naïve or not, I'm just finished!" Ava insisted.

Daniel shook his elegantly graying head. "No. It's not that easy."

"Not easy—but true."

Daniel stared hard at Ava. "It's fitting, that I thought of *Breakfast at Tiffany's* when I happened upon you today," he said. "I don't know if you've ever read Capote's book, but in a way, you and Holly Golightly are a lot alike. Secret pasts, a glamorous façade, a double life. And just as she couldn't wangle her way out of her commitments, neither can you."

Ava wasn't completely following Daniel's logic; all she knew was that the freedom she'd felt these last few days seemed to be disappearing under a bank of storm clouds.

Daniel continued. "I'm not some nobody in this city. I don't mean to be immodest, but I'm a powerful man in circles that could make or break your newfound happiness, Ava. Walk away if you want, but you should know that there will be consequences."

"What kind of *consequences*?" Ava asked miserably. She really didn't want to know.

"Let's just say, when you're through with me, you'll be through in this town."

Ava felt like she'd been socked in the stomach. Daniel looked at her, his face suddenly filled with concern. "Come on, sweetheart. Don't look so miserable. It'll all work out. And I don't want to keep you from whomever you've dressed up so prettily for. We don't have to solve anything now. But I insist we meet again to put things to bed," he said slyly. "Shall we say Friday? Two o'clock at our usual spot?"

Even when Daniel was issuing a threat, his whole aura was alluring. Ava felt like she was being seduced, just as she had when she'd gotten involved with Daniel in the first place. With a heavy heart she agreed to the meeting. Daniel kissed her once more on the cheek and then disappeared inside Bergdorf's.

Ava glanced at her watch. It was a quarter to six— her date with Reese was moments away. Only now, everything was different. Ava's newfound freedom had slipped away. She got on the subway and headed down-town for another night alone in her dorm. There would be no date.

8
The Bronx Kicks Ass

"READY TO SHOOT SOME street style, love?"

Sam Owens stuck his head inside the intern office. Nadine could feel herself blushing—again. This was not like her. She didn't lose her shit over guys, even guys as utterly hot as Sam. And calling her "love" didn't mean anything, either, she told herself. Sam was English. They all talked like that.

"I was just cleaning my lenses," Nadine explained. "I'm bringing film and digital today."

"Clever girl. Here's your coffee." He handed over a Venti iced cappuccino, the plastic cup sweating in the morning heat. "So, ever been to the Bronx?"

"Nah, but my peeps are from North Philly, so I don't scare easily."

"The Bronx gets a bad rap," Sam said, his blue eyes crinkling with laughter. "It's huge, for one. And even the dodgy parts are no worse than Brixton."

"Brixton, that's in London, right? There's a Clash song about it."

Sam smiled again. "'Guns of Brixton.' No quicker way to steal a lad's heart than quoting the Clash."

At that, Nadine's own heart did a little leap. *Calm down,* she told herself. This was the same guy whose tux she'd puked on. This was the guy who was also one of the hottest photographers in the city. This was the guy she'd thrown herself at, only to be turned down, albeit very politely. He was clearly not interested in a kid like her. But he was just so damn nice. It was hard *not* to let her imagination get the best of her.

Nadine and Sam made their way to the Sixth Avenue subway station. As the train thundered uptown, Sam explained that he was taking her to the Fordham area. Grand Concourse, he said, had a good mix of black, Afro-Caribbean, and Latino people. "So you get this fantastic blend of styles and influences. I doubt you'll catch many formal getups here, but I think you'll definitely find similarities between the grass-roots style and this fall's collections." Sam went on to name several designers who Nadine had never heard of.

Nadine listened attentively, feeling like a bit of an idiot. Even though the whole Bling Couture thing had been her idea, she wasn't aware of half the stuff Sam was talking about. She was also finding it a little hard to pay attention, as busy as she was tallying Sam's selling points: Not only was he a fox, not only was he a decent guy, not only was he a great photographer—he also had a thorough understanding of fashion. No wonder he was such a bigwig at the ripe old age of twenty-three.

As soon as they exited the train at Fordham Road, Nadine completely lost herself. Though she'd been lugging her cameras around for the last few weeks, taking shots of the other interns and of Manhattan, nothing had juiced her up the way that the frenetic street life of the Bronx did. There were people everywhere, and the smells of foods—barbecue from one store, Jamaican roti from another—wafted through the streets. Hip-hop and salsa music thumped from stores and cars. Old men hung out on stoops playing dominoes. Packs of teenage girls sashayed down the streets in skintight jeans and teeny-tiny tank tops, one layered on top of the other. Nadine got out her camera and started shooting.

"Hey, baby, you want me to smile pretty for you?" a group of teenage boys asked her.

Nadine just laughed and clicked away. She was skipping up Grand Concourse, almost forgetting that Sam was even there, but when she stopped to change memory cards, she noticed him watching her.

"What?" she asked him. "Am I screwing up?"

"On the contrary. You're a natural. Mind if I see what you've got so far?"

Nadine handed Sam her camera and watched anxiously as he clicked through the shots. Her mom liked to say that ice water ran through Nadine's veins and nothing ever ruffled her—but waiting for Sam's approval she was downright rattled.

Sam nodded his head. "Just as I figured."

"What?" Nadine asked.

"You've got a great eye, both for subjects and for composition. You've been firing away with this camera and still you've managed to get an inordinately large number of great shots."

"Really?" Nadine asked. "I mean, I feel like I haven't even been looking at the fashion angle. I'm just so energized that I'm snapping everything I see."

"But that's the best way to shoot. It's organic. And I already see a number of things you can use in your pitch. See that cute Latina girl with the chain-link belt? Well, I recall from the Eamon Sinds collection, there's a whole lot of mesh going on. And of course chained jeans are huge this fall."

"Wow. I didn't even put that together," Nadine said.

"Of course you did," Sam replied. "The way you shoot pictures is so intuitive—it's what makes you a true photographer."

In the past, whenever anyone complimented Nadine on being a good photographer (or writer, or student, or whatever) her standard reply was "Damn straight." But she was so genuinely flattered by what Sam had said, so completely overwhelmed, that she didn't say anything. In fact, what Nadine really wanted to do was march up to Sam, grab his adorably scruffy face, and pull it down to meet her lips. But Sam had made his feelings clear.

They spent the next two hours shooting all around the neighborhood, stopping to grab some grilled chicken and rice from a street vendor. Around four thirty, Sam glanced at his Swiss Army watch. "Ahh, bollocks. I've got to get back to Manhattan. I'm meeting someone at six."

Nadine had the feeling that *someone* was a date. She tried to swallow her jealousy. On the train back downtown, Sam chattered on about his job at *Couture*. What it was like to shoot fashion shows versus studio versus location. He was so easygoing and nice, and Nadine really felt that they might become friends. But for that to happen, she had to clear the air about gala night.

"Listen, Sam. I've owed you an apology for about a week now."

Sam raised a brow. "What'd you do? Steal my beer or something?"

"You're being very nice about it, but I made a total ass of myself at the gala."

Sam cocked his head to the side and grinned. "You weren't in your best form," he admitted.

"Please. I was completely wasted and feeling sorry for myself for a whole bunch of ridiculous shit. And I was totally inappropriate with you. It's just, I thought—"

"You thought what?"

"I guess I'm not used to guys being nice for no reason, you know, without wanting something in return."

Sam frowned. "Let's get this straight. I neither want nor expect anything in return."

"I know. I get that now," Nadine said. "And I'm so mortified that I threw up on your jacket. You have to at least let me pay for the dry cleaning."

"I wouldn't hear of it," Sam said.

"But you gotta let me make it up to you somehow," Nadine offered.

"Tell you what. When you publish your first book of photographs, you just remember me in the acknowledgments."

"You got yourself a deal," Nadine said, grinning.

Sam had to get off the train at Columbus Circle for his drinks thing, so Nadine decided to jump off with him and walk toward Fifth Avenue on her way back to *Couture*.

"Thanks so much for today," Nadine said. "The Bronx kicks ass!"

"You should sell that slogan to the mayor," Sam replied. "And, you know, it strikes me that I still owe you a shoot. We're shooting a beauty story at the Clementine Gallery in Chelsea the day after tomorrow. Care to come?"

Nadine suppressed the urge to fling herself at Sam and wrap her arms around his wiry waist. Instead she just smiled and said she'd love to.

"Excellent," he said with a wave as he set off down 58th Street toward the Hudson Hotel. As Nadine watched him go, she wished he had kissed her—just a friendly peck on the cheek, even. Didn't everyone in

New York do that? But then, halfway down the block, as if he knew she had been watching him, Sam turned around and flashed a grin at her, making Nadine's heart do that skipping thing again.

She flipped open her phone to call Aynsley and got her voice mail. "Let's do some serious partying tonight," she said. She'd had a great day and wanted to celebrate. And maybe flirting with someone else would help get Sam off her mind.

Fifth Avenue was mobbed with tourists converging on Tiffany's and FAO Schwarz, so it took Nadine ages just to thread through a few blocks. She was about to give up and head back over to Sixth Avenue when she did a double take. There, in front of Bergdorf's, was Ava's Silver Fox. And he was talking with Miss Ava herself.

Nadine slouched down into the crowd and sneaked up closer. Ava claimed that this guy was just some designer she'd been interviewing. But the first time Nadine had seen them together, having drinks on the patio at Palais, they'd had their heads together, all conspiratorial. It didn't look like any professional lunch Nadine had ever had.

And it didn't look professional today, either. Ava and this guy were obviously having a disagreement of some sort. He had a stern expression on his face, and Ava was waving her hands in the air, her eyes darting back and forth as if looking for an escape. As Nadine got a little closer, it was plain to see that Ava was on the verge of tears.

A clothing designer, my ass, Nadine thought. Nadine knew a lover's quarrel when she saw one. And no way was she gonna let Ava off the hook with some bullshit excuse about interviewing this guy. This time Nadine was gonna get herself some proof. She pulled a camera out of her bag and quickly attached the zoom lens. Then she zeroed in on Ava and the Silver Fox and clicked away. She kept clicking until the guy kissed Ava on the cheek and Ava took off down Fifth Avenue.

Nadine ducked west on 56th Street and didn't look up until she was sure that Ava was out of sight. It had been a day of discoveries, all of them safely stored on her camera. Nadine patted her camera bag like it was a faithful cat and then skipped all the way back to *Couture*.

"I don't mind living in a man's world as long as I can be a woman in it." —Marilyn Monroe

Filed under: Fashionista > Style

In many ways, the Fashionista agrees wholeheartedly with the fabulous <u>Ms. Monroe</u>. Personally, I would happily spend my whole life in a world populated by the likes of <u>Nicolas Ghesquière</u>, the genius behind <u>Balenciaga</u> (and Nic, if you're reading, I can't wait to wear my new <u>cranberry velvet-lapeled smoking jacket</u> this fall); <u>Alber Elbaz</u> (the genius behind <u>Lanvin</u>, who the Fashionista thanks for the fabulously sexy <u>black trench coat</u> she just bought); and <u>Christian Louboutin</u> (the Fashionista's feet love you!).

But the Fashionista also knows that the world has changed in ways that Marilyn would find quite » pleasing. Alongside Nic, Alber, and Christian, we have <u>Stella McCartney</u>, <u>Miuccia Prada</u>, <u>Diane Von Furstenberg</u>, <u>Donna Karan</u>, <u>Jil Sander</u>, and the divine duo behind <u>Marchesa</u>, <u>Georgina Chapman and Keren Craig</u>, to name but a few. Women top the mastheads of almost every fashion magazine in the world, and they claim corner offices in a good number of multinational fashion companies, too.

Marilyn, it's not *just* a man's world anymore, but some less-than-exemplary males are still messing around in it. The Fashionista is constantly surprised at the ways in which a man—rich, powerful, supposedly intelligent—can still be led by what's in his impeccably pressed <u>Prada pants</u>, rather than what's between the ears that hold up his <u>Armani shades</u>. Boys will be boys, I suppose. But aren't boys supposed to eventually become men? Ponder that . . . until next time.

Your faithful Fashionista

9
Your Last Dying Wish

WHOEVER SAID THAT THE waiting is the hardest part was
a complete idiot.

For the last week Callie had endured constant abuse
at the office, in addition to the indignity of knowing
that Aynsley had caught her red-handed in Julian's
bedroom. Yet neither of those experiences had her as
freaked out as the prospect of meeting with Quinn and
Marceline. When she'd called Quinn late last week to
discuss the next steps, he was the one who recommended a joint meeting. Callie had agreed to it. She
hadn't had much of a choice, really.

She'd expected Marceline to question why a lowly

intern like Callie was asking for her time. But, instead, Marceline had just smiled and told her to set something up with her assistant. On Friday the appointment was scheduled to take place today—*Tuesday*—and Callie had spent the entire weekend obsessing about it. She'd been unable to think of anything else. She scarcely slept. And when she did close her eyes, her dreams were all surreal visions of the impending meeting. In one she was buck naked. In the other, she walked in on Quinn and Marceline making out.

She couldn't take much more of the unknown. Any more waiting and she was sure she was going to go insane.

"Marceline is ready for you now," said Blythe, her model-like assistant.

Callie gulped and smoothed her black-and-white Forever 21 bubble dress. Somehow, it would have been wrong to wear her own designs today. Quinn stood up and grabbed a sheaf of paperwork. Callie had no idea what it contained: legal documents? Affidavits? Whatever they were, they surely spelled doom for Callie's career.

They stepped into Marceline's cramped office, lit-tered with handbags, shoes, wallets, and other accessories. Her computer monitor was up, revealing the latest Fashionista blog. Marceline was on the phone and seemed to be discussing the latest blog gossip. She motioned for Callie and Quinn to sit down, then hung up and smiled a toothy grin.

"So, Quinn, is it? Are you a friend of Callie's from Ohio?"

Quinn looked deeply offended by this assumption, which Callie found annoying. "Um, no," Quinn said. "I'm from Brooklyn."

Marceline looked confused. "Oh, I thought Callie wanted me to meet a designer friend of hers from home."

"Um, Quinn's a designer," Callie replied. "But we're not friends." She felt nauseous. She knew her ugliest secret was about to come out, but she hoped it wasn't accompanied by the contents of her stomach. Not that there was much in there—she'd been subsisting on Diet Coke for the last few days.

"I design hats," Quinn said. "But I do silk screens, as well."

Marceline furrowed her perfectly plucked brows. "Oh, so did you teach Callie how to silk-screen? She made the most fabulous bags for us out of—"

"Dead celebrities," Quinn interjected.

"Why yes," Marceline said. "You must've seen an

advance issue of the Cutting Edge Showcase."

"I did," Quinn said, staring at Callie. He wasn't going to make this easy on her by doing the talking. She took a deep breath and jumped in.

"Quinn was the one who made the silk screens," she blurted.

"Pardon?" Marceline said.

"The silk screens are his."

"You mean you worked on them together?" Marceline asked.

Why was she being so dense? Did she want to make this as hard for Callie as possible?

"No. We didn't make them together. I bought the silk screens from him in his Williamsburg store and I made the bags using his fabric."

"So did you work out a licensing agreement?"

"No," Callie said, her voice barely a whisper.

Marceline's gray eyes narrowed as the true purpose of the meeting dawned on her. "And you didn't know that she was using your designs for her bags?" she asked Quinn.

"No idea," Quinn replied. "I thought she was just some kid who wanted the silk screens to hang on her bedroom wall. I didn't know what she was using the fabric for until I saw my work in *Couture*, attributed to the 'wunderkind designer' that *you* had discovered."

Marceline sighed deeply and pinched the bridge of her nose, muttering obscenities to herself. "I think we need to get Kiki in on this. Isabel's in Europe right now." Marceline picked up her phone, and Callie could hear Kiki objecting on the other end, until Marceline said, "We might be in deep shit, thanks to one of your interns, so get your ass down here."

It was then that Callie understood that waiting for this shoe to fall had been a cakewalk compared to the feeling as it hit her—heel down—directly on the head. She suddenly comprehended the full weight of her situation. How the hell had she gotten herself into this mess? She hadn't told anyone that she made the material. It had seemed like such an innocent omission. But now, Marceline couldn't even look at her, and Kiki was storming into the office, red-faced with fury.

"What the hell is going on?" she demanded.

As Marceline and Quinn filled Kiki in, Callie floated out of her body. This couldn't really be happening to her. It was all a dream. Except that she couldn't wake herself up. Not even when Kiki turned to her, guns blazing.

"Do you realize the situation you've put the magazine in?" she barked.

Callie didn't know what to say. She stared at her sandals.

"Well, let me illuminate," Kiki said snidely. "*Couture* is *the* bible of high fashion because people believe in what we have to say. When we tell them that teal is the new black, they wear teal. When we say stacked-heel oxfords are all the rage, they rush to be the first to trot down their block in a pair. And when we say that we've discovered a promising young designer who *not only* makes a great handbag but also creates *her own* unique fabric, and we then honor this person at our exclusive gala, our readers believe it's more than hype. They trust that the seventeen-year-old is an up-and-coming designer—*not a thief!*"

"But I didn't steal anything. I designed the bags myself," Callie said weakly. Hadn't Ava told her that the design was what mattered?

"Do you realize," Kiki continued, hardly acknowledging that Callie had spoken, "that you have managed to single-handedly sully *Couture*'s reputation, and that you've placed the magazine in legal jeopardy as well—depending on how Mr. McGrath here decides to proceed?"

"I didn't mean to pass the silk screens off as my own," Callie cried. "It was just that you all assumed that they were mine and you were so excited about the purses and getting my designs in *Couture* has always been my dream and I was just so overwhelmed—"

"Callie," Kiki interrupted. "I don't care if getting a bag in *Couture* was your last dying wish. What you've done is beyond the pale, and I'm insulted that you're trying to justify it."

"I'm sorry" was all Callie could manage to whimper.

"Well, you should be," Kiki continued. "You are hereby suspended from your internship at *Couture*. I'd fire you myself, but it's not my call. I have to speak to Isabel and she's currently incommunicado on Donatella's yacht. Once I've spoken with her, and Mr. McGrath here, and our lawyers, and our publicists, *then* you and I will talk."

"But what about the contest?" Callie asked. She'd finally come up with an idea she was excited about. It was a round-up of earth-conscious fashion designs called How Green Is Your Runway?

"Aynsley can present your idea, Callie. Now please excuse us. We have important matters to discuss."

Callie was grateful that she'd at least managed to keep herself together until after she'd exited Marceline's office. She made it to the ladies' room, ran into the last stall, and buried her head in her hands and sobbed. Two weeks ago, she'd been the toast of the town, on an upward fashion trajectory, and dating Julian Rothwell, one of the hottest, richest guys in the city. But today, she was a nobody again. No—worse than that: a nobody on the verge of being a laughing-stock, one step away from being fired. And the cherry on top of her humiliation cake: Aynsley had most certainly told Julian her other harmless little lie. By now he must have learned that she wasn't a prep-school heiress but just a regular old middle-class girl from Ohio.

Callie cried until her hiccups subsided. She splashed cold water on her face, reapplied her mascara, and put on her knockoff Fendi aviator shades. Then she sneaked out of the offices. She couldn't bear to face the other interns, not even Ava.

Outside, the morning was incongruously pretty. Deep blue skies, eighty-five degrees, the air refreshingly dry. It was the perfect kind of day to spend wandering through Central Park or cruising the boutiques in Nolita. But Callie had no desire to tool around. She felt as if the entire city was laughing at her now. Not the people, but the city itself—chuckling at stupid little

Country Callie, who'd been deluded enough to think that she could make it in Manhattan. Fat chance of that.

She took the subway downtown, and back at the dorm, she went to her mailbox, hoping for a letter from home or one of her celebrity magazines—something to distract here from her troubles. But there was nothing in her cubby except a flyer for car insurance and a Visa bill.

Upstairs, she grabbed a Diet Coke from her mini-fridge and sat down to look at her bill. When she saw the total, she nearly fainted. Somehow, she'd managed to block out all the things she'd bought last month. But there was the damage: $2,643.59. Her Bergdorf's outfit alone was nearly $2,000. And then there were all those great deals she just couldn't pass up—the pants from H&M, that upscale consignment store dress, those Marc Jacobs slingbacks from Century 21—of course it all added up, but she'd barely thought about it. It was like, with every purchase, she'd bought her own rich girl lie, but that fantasy had just collided with an ugly dose of reality. The total balance due was almost twice the amount of spending money her parents had given her for the entire summer. *Where the hell was she going to get that kind of cash?*

Callie had to figure something out fast, because if

her parents found out how much she'd charged up, their response would make Kiki's outrage look positively mild. And *really*, if there was one thing Callie couldn't afford, it was more drama.

10

Proof

NADINE WAS IMPRESSED WITH herself. Not just in her usual *ain't-I-the-shit?* kind of way, but genuinely pleased with the caliber of work she'd produced on her shoot in the Bronx. After printing up a dozen of her favorite digital shots from her Mac, she'd slipped into the darkroom to develop the best of the film pics. Sam had already picked up her negatives from the lab, and he'd circled his favorites with a wax pencil. And wouldn't you know it? Sam's favorites were Nadine's favorites, too. Not that she'd tell him that. She already felt like a swoony teenager around him, and though at eighteen, Nadine Van Buren qualified as teenaged, she took pride in what she considered her sophisticated, early-twenties vibe.

Throwing a Linkin Park CD into the darkroom player, Nadine cranked the volume and danced around the tiny room. She put her negatives into the enlarger and futzed around with shading to give the pics an edgy, out-of-focus look. When she was satisfied with her test prints, she ran a series of eight-by-tens and watched them materialize in the chemicals. As usual, when she was in the darkroom, Nadine completely lost track of time. She didn't even realize it was lunchtime until her stomach started growling.

She checked her watch. It was one o'clock. In two hours, she had to be in Chelsea at the Clementine Gallery for the beauty shoot Sam had invited her to. She was beyond psyched to be Sam's assistant—and ridiculously jazzed that he had also agreed to shoot the fabulous silver lamé suit that Ava had picked up at Bergdorf's. Best yet, one of the *Couture* girls—a model who owed Sam a favor—was going to pose in the suit, free of charge.

Nadine's gut let out an angry growl. "Oh, simmer down," she said aloud. "No time to eat. I got work to do."

Nadine already had plenty of great shots to include

in her Bling Couture presentation tomorrow, but she had one last important piece of business to attend to. She pulled out the only roll of film she hadn't given to Sam to develop, which contained a bunch of pics of Ava and the Silver Fox in front of Bergdorf's. Nadine didn't really need to make prints. The negatives were evidence enough that something was going on with Miss Innocent and her older man. But there was something about developing an image that made what Nadine had seen more than just some figment of her imagination. Photos were hard-core proof.

It was the same reason that, a few weeks ago, Nadine had printed out a shot of her and Julian in an, *um*, compromising position. Someone had taken Nadine's camera and snapped a picture of her and Julian in the middle of a lip-lock on one of Cecilia Rothwell's hideous floral couches. Nadine didn't remember many details about partying with the socialite set at the Rothwells' that night, but the picture itself seemed to offer a clue about an otherwise blurry evening. So she'd made a print of the kiss as a souvenir, and then promptly hid the smoking-gun photo at the bottom of her dorm room drawer. She knew Callie would have a type-A conniption if she saw it—and the girl seemed to have enough problems already.

As Nadine developed her last shots, she once again couldn't help but be impressed. Not with her skills—these pics weren't artful—but with Ava. She'd managed to work her whole like-a-virgin act so convincingly, all the while sneaking around with this piece of finely aged prime hottie. Sure, Ava was pretty, but this guy was gorgeous, and *clearly* rich and powerful. In other words, way out of Ava's league. Then again, maybe Mr. Big was trying to shake her off, and Ava was making a last-ditch attempt to keep from being tossed like last year's Sevens. She sure hoped Ava didn't have any happily-ever-after hopes for this guy. She just seemed so vulnerable. Nadine didn't want her to get hurt.

At this point, Nadine's stomach was growling loudly. "All right, already," she said. "I'll feed you." She took off the oversized T-shirt she'd donned to keep from mussing her (or make that Aynsley's) champagne-colored Dolce & Gabbana dress. Then she gathered up the Bronx shots and the Silver Fox series and stashed them in her Coach python tote bag (also Aynsley's).

Downstairs, in Conrad Media's see-and-be-seen cafeteria, she passed up the high-heeled masses waiting in line for the sushi bar and the salad station. The grill was empty, as usual, so Nadine ordered a double cheeseburger and fries and wolfed them down before heading to the ladies' room for a quick freshen-up. She put a bit of Bed Head in her hair, which she wore short and natural today because Sam had mentioned that the style suited her, and capped off her look with a pair of diva-esque white sunglasses, for a touch of Van Buren 'tude. "Ready as you'll ever be," she told her reflection.

When Nadine arrived at Clementine Gallery, it was a chaotic scene. She was ignored by two models, a fashion stylist, a beauty stylist, two makeup artists, and a PR rep. Then she caught a glimpse of Sam, who looked even cuter than usual in his ripped-up Levi's, faded oxford shirt, and Converse high-tops. As Nadine watched everyone scurry back and forth, she felt like a third wheel—or make that a ninth wheel. She wasn't exactly sure what to do, so she grabbed a strawberry off the catering table and hung back against the big picture window. Sam was too busy setting up the lighting to notice her anyway.

Nadine watched the models as they had their hair and makeup done. Every time she saw one of these mannequins walking through *Couture*'s hallways, she couldn't help but admire their beauty—and wonder what planet they came from. Models were mutants:

giraffe-girls, with no boobs, no hips, and cheekbones that could cut steak (not that they'd eat it). And today's specimens were no different. There was Anezka, a tomboyish-looking Czech who'd single-handedly started a floppy short hair sensation when she hacked off her butt-length blond locks. And next to her was one of Nadine's all-time favorite models: Zehna, the most beautiful glamazon this side of Iman. Zehna was over six feet tall, with coffee-brown skin, a swanlike neck, and intense green eyes, which were currently being powdered with a palette of teal and blue.

"Lovely, isn't she?"

Nadine looked up into Sam's grinning face. "Beyond gorgeous," Nadine replied. It was so true that she wasn't even jealous to hear Sam say it.

"I love how the colors play so differently on the two girls. Zehna's going to be modeling your suit, by the way."

"Zehna? Are you serious?" Nadine shrieked.

"Did someone use my name in vain?" Zehna asked in a lilting Ethiopian accent.

"Hello, love," Sam said. "This is Nadine Van Buren. My protégé."

Zehna raised an eyebrow. "Your protégé, is it? Nice to meet you, Nadine. Love that dress. D&G? I've got the same one in purple."

"Uh, yeah," Nadine said, beyond tongue-tied.

"Zehna, get your ass back here!" the makeup artist shouted, sending her back to the director's chair set up in front of a panel of three mirrors.

"Okay then, do you have any experience with reflectors?" Sam asked, holding up a circular screen in front of Nadine.

"A little bit," she admitted.

"Don't worry. I'll show you what to do. The shoot should take about two hours, so we'll have some nice late-afternoon light left when you shoot Zehna for the Bling Couture piece."

"*I'm* shooting *Zehna?*" Nadine asked. "Are you sure . . . I mean maybe you should . . ."

"No arguments. I have every confidence that you'll do a stunning job. After seeing your Bronx work, I can tell you have an innate sense of good lighting. That's something that can't be learned."

Nadine felt her face warm with pleasure, so she busied herself with unpacking cameras and equipment, lest Sam see her blush. When she'd composed herself, she asked Sam to put her to work. She prepped the film, took light meter readings, and hung tinted plastic sheets over the windows to give the room a rosy glow.

At four o'clock, when the afternoon light was streaming through the west-facing windows, they got started.

As soon as the cameras started clicking and the
flashes started popping, Nadine forgot her nervousness.
She grooved to the great mix Sam had made—James
Brown one minute, Björk the next. Everyone was
laughing, dancing, and prancing around, Anezka and
Zehna playing off each other, teasing each other, cracking jokes. There wasn't a whiff of catfight in the air.

Before she knew it, the beauty shoot was over, and
in front of everyone, Anezka stripped naked and
changed into a frayed denim miniskirt and a beat-up
Led Zeppelin T-shirt. Then she plunked down in the
corner and started chain-smoking Camel Lights.
Zehna, who'd disappeared into the back of the room,
returned wearing the silver bling couture suit—and it
looked a thousand times better on her than it had on the
hanger. The gold tones in her skin and eyes really made
the metallic material pop. The hairstylist had slicked
her kinky mane straight back in a sophisticated
chignon. The makeup artist, however, had gone all
disco glam: blue sparkles on her eyes, streaks of crimson
across her cheeks. Her hair and makeup typified the
precise street-style, high-fashion juxtaposition that
Nadine and Ava had been going for.

"You're up," Sam said, handing Nadine a camera.

Her hands were shaking as she took the Canon. Sam grabbed her wrist and steadied it. "You'll do fine. It's no different here than it was in the Bronx. Just do your thing."

Nadine took a couple of Polaroid test shots and, when she was satisfied with the lighting, she got started. Just like in the darkroom earlier that day, Nadine soon forgot where she was, forgot who she was shooting, forgot who was standing behind her watching—not just Sam, but Anezka and the two stylists who'd hung back to watch her in action. By the time she'd shot three rolls, she was sweating and out of breath—and more exhilarated than she'd been in her entire life.

"Shall we take a look at the digitals?" Zehna asked. "Just a tiny peek."

"You know it's never a good idea for a model to see unedited work." Sam laughed.

"Oh, is good idea," Anezka said between puffs of her cigarette. "The girl is learning. We offer good advisement."

"Good advisement, eh?" Sam said. "You mind if we all take a look?" he asked, turning to Nadine.

Nadine felt like she was floating. "Sure. Whatever," she said.

Sam plugged her memory card into his Mac laptop and beckoned her over. Nadine shook her head. She wasn't ready to look at the shots yet. It was still sinking in that she'd just shot a fashion story. Besides, she was a little terrified to witness Sam's reaction. Today, all the bravado in the world wasn't going to prove anything. Only her work could save her now.

So Nadine grabbed a Poland Spring off the catering table and pretended to drink as she watched Sam and the models out of the corner of her eye. Sam was impossible to read, his face a mask of deep concentration. Anezka seemed bored, blowing smoke rings at the monitor. But then she turned to Nadine and said, "When we come together again, you remember to shoot left."

"Huh?" Nadine asked.

"What Anezka means," Zehna explained, "is when you're a hot fashion photographer—and you're obviously on your way—please remember that her left side is her best side. But the girl is crazy—she's a babe from any angle."

"I'm not a crazy," Anezka shot back.

Zehna laughed. "Yes you are. And your English is apalling."

"Oh, shut up. You are just jealous because I got

mentioned by the Fashionista," Anezka said with a smile.

"*Please*, she named a skinny blonde from the Czech Republic. That could be anyone. But, if she'd mentioned a beautiful African—well, then there'd be no question."

"She write about skinny blond model from Czech Republic with short hair and killer style. Of course this is me," Anezka replied with a mischievous grin.

Zehna and Anezka kept up their debate as they looked through Nadine's shots, but Sam stood still and quiet.

"What?" Nadine finally blurted. "Say something. Even if you hate them."

"I don't hate them, Nadine," Sam said, still staring at the screen.

"Okay, they're mediocre, right? Not *Couture* enough?"

"As if you could do mediocre." Sam finally broke away from the monitor. "These are excellent, Nadine. Even better than I'd hoped."

Zehna and Anezka whooped in delight. "The master approves," they crowed. "A star is born."

"We must win her to our side, early," Anezka said.

"Absolutely," Zehna agreed.

"We start tonight. We go to fabulous new bar called Halcyon. You come party with us," Anezka insisted.

"*Seriously?*" Nadine couldn't believe it. Not only had she just shot a supermodel, but now she was going to party like one! Her luck had done a complete 180.

"Of course," Zehna said. "Work time is over. Party time is starting."

"I'm there," Nadine crowed. "Come on. Let's go celebrate."

Outside, the streets of West Chelsea were dead. They walked to Tenth Avenue and Anezka stuck out her slender arm to hail a cab. Five taxis promptly screeched to a halt. Anezka stamped out her tenth cigarette in an hour and jumped into one of them. Zehna followed. But Nadine looked to Sam. "You ridin' shotgun?"

Sam shook his head. "Ah, no. I think I'll take a pass."

"But you gotta come with us!" Nadine cried. "It's my big night!"

Sam smiled. "You girls go have fun. I'll get your prints ready for tomorrow's presentation."

"But I can do that in the morning—the presentation isn't until after lunch. Are you sure you don't want to come?" Nadine knew she sounded desperate, but she really wanted Sam with her tonight. Not *just* because she had the serious hots for him, but because he was so much a part of today's triumph. But before she had a chance to insist, Sam waved good-bye and jumped into a cab of his own.

"That man never come out with us," Anezka said.

"It's why he's the best," Zehna defended. "He doesn't live for the party."

Nadine tried to swallow her disappointment. She didn't get Sam at all. He was a nice guy who helped her for the sake of it? A hotshot photographer who turned down partying with models?

"I don't know for that. He probably has date. Never mind him," Anezka said, lighting two cigarettes at once and handing one to Nadine.

Nadine didn't normally smoke, but she didn't *normally* party with supermodels, either. And hey, maybe a little smoke would snuff out the image of Sam canoodling with some other girl. She accepted the cigarette and inhaled deeply. Then she reached into her Coach bag for her lipstick and felt the hard metal of her Canon Elph. She'd forgotten she had the camera with her. Good thing, because a night like tonight was definitely gonna require some proof.

11

Green Is the New Black

WHERE THE HELL WAS the little twit?

Aynsley paced the intern office, trying to calm her nerves and quell her anger. Callie, her unofficial office bitch, had been MIA since Tuesday afternoon. And in one hour, they had their fashion-feature presentation—the one that Callie was *supposed* to be in charge of. But this morning, the lying phony had emailed Aynsley a text version of the proposal and a vague message about how Aynsley might have to present for the both of them. The idea—*How Green Is Your Runway?*—wasn't half bad. It definitely nailed a hot trend. Even the most conspicuous consumers these days bragged about offsetting their carbon footprint by investing in some organic coffee plantation in Honduras or whatever. But Callie hadn't fleshed out the concept. All Aynsley had was a five-page memo. No photos. No samples. And now, no Callie.

"Shit," Aynsley said as she smoothed her white Lanvin zippered halter dress. "That little bitch has left me in the lurch."

Not that Aynsley cared much about *winning* the contest. After all, she hadn't done a single thing to help. It was more about keeping up appearances, making it look like she'd put in some effort. At the very least, she needed her parents to think that she'd tried. Oh well, she had an hour to think on it. And she knew at least enough about the fashion scene to know which designers were gearing up to go green. She'd wing it in the meeting and do fine.

"Hey, Sly, got time for lunch before the presentation?" Nadine asked. Her friend had just emerged from an epic stint in the darkroom, and her eyes were tinged with red. Whether it was from the chemicals or last night's booze-fest, Aynsley couldn't be sure. She hadn't been included in Nadine's little model outing—so at least she wasn't as hungover as the competition.

"What, don't you want to do some last-minute strategizing with Ava?" Aynsley prodded.

"Nah, we're cool," Nadine said, refusing to take the bait. "At least I think we are. I don't know where Ava is."

"That makes two no-shows. Callie's not coming in, apparently," Aynsley sighed. "Such hassles in my life. But still, a girl does have to eat—and I've got a yen for spicy tuna roll."

"Ugh, don't even mention sushi," Nadine begged, looking a little green. "Noodle soup is probably all I can stomach."

"You shouldn't drink so much, Van Buren," Aynsley teased.

"I know. I know," Nadine lamented. "It was just those girls. How can they put away so much booze, still be so damn thin, and get up for their ten a.m. calls?"

"Easy. They don't eat. They snort coke."

"Zehna doesn't do that shit," Nadine interrupted. "Don't be dissin' my girl."

"She's your girl now, is she?" Aynsley shot back with a grin. "Anyhow, the big models never make their calls; they're always late. And if we don't want to be, we better hit the caf now."

As they made their way to the elevator banks,

Aynsley eyed Nadine's outfit. The girl looked like she was trying to channel Rihanna, but the result was a mess. She was wearing a plaid suit, so busy that it made Aynsley reach for her shades. Her skirt barely skimmed her thighs, and her jacket—underneath which she wore nothing but skin—was cut to her navel. Circling her waist was at least a pound's worth of gold chain, and there was plenty more hardware around her neck. She'd even wrapped a turban on her head.

"I see you dressed down for the presentation," Aynsley said with a smirk.

"Oh, *this?*" Nadine said, running her hand down her side with a flourish. "This is just part of the package. You'll see."

During lunch, Aynsley did her best to tune out Nadine's endless prattle about yesterday's shoot: how cool the models were, how nice Sam was—not to mention endless musings on why Sam didn't go out with them, blab blab-blab blab blab. In her head, Aynsley practiced her pitch to Isabel, Dieter, and Kiki. She wasn't going to get too worked up about it. No matter how well prepped Ava and Nadine might be, Aynsley knew that she could talk rings around both of them even on her worst day.

At one thirty they went back upstairs. Ava was

waiting in the intern office, looking elegant in a beige Calvin Klein pantsuit. Aynsley couldn't help but notice the thick dossier that she carried as part of her presentation.

"You guys ready?" Ava asked with a tense smile.

"It's not 'you guys.' Just me. Callie's not here," Aynsley responded. Even though Callie and Ava were on different teams for the concept contest, they'd remained thick as thieves. But Ava appeared to be just as shocked as Aynsley about Callie's no-show.

"I don't know what's going on," Ava replied. "I haven't talked to her all week. She's not answering her door or her cell phone."

"It must be serious for her to forgo an opportunity to kiss editor ass," Nadine quipped.

"Who's kissing my ass?" Kiki asked from the doorway. "Come on, ladies, time to face the music. Isabel just returned from Europe and she's been putting out fires all morning, so let's make this brief."

Nadine, Ava, and Aynsley filed into the conference room. Isabel and Dieter were already there, looking stone-faced. Aynsley wondered if she'd have to make excuses for Callie; in fact, it felt like divine justice. All last week, Callie had been covering for Aynsley, and now the tables had turned. Although, looking around the room, no one seemed surprised that Callie was missing. In fact, Kiki turned to Aynsley and informed her that she'd be giving a solo presentation in Callie's absence.

"Where *is* Callie, exactly?" Aynsley asked. If the bosses knew something she didn't, why not put the onus on them to explain? Besides, better for them to think that Aynsley was clueless—and blameless for any deficits in their presentation.

"Uh, well," Kiki began. "Callie has had a little . . ."

"Callie is on a special project and she won't be coming in for the next few days," Isabel interrupted with a stern look. Kiki immediately buttoned her lip.

Aynsley smelled a lie. If Callie had scored some special assignment, the faker would have been gloating instead of hiding. After all, she was genetically incapable of keeping her mouth shut. But Aynsley didn't have much time to ponder the possibilities before Kiki turned to her and said, "You're up."

Aynsley stood, and then, summoning confidence from the bottom of her white Gucci slides to the top of her freshly coiffed head, she announced, "Green is the new black. Leonardo DiCaprio, Cameron Diaz, Julia Roberts—for years these celebs have been driving around in hybrid cars, transforming their Beverly Hills mansions into eco-friendly paradises, and hobnobbing with Al Gore. And finally, the fashion world is catching on. Organic fabrics aren't just for ugly, hemp-wearing hippies anymore." Aynsley went on for the next ten minutes, making, *she thought*, a rather persuasive case for her concept. She'd dropped more names than *People* magazine and Isabel seemed duly impressed. *Who knew?* Maybe she had a shot at winning this thing after all.

But then Ava and Nadine stood up, opened their file, and spread out a series of photos, including a mock-up spread called Bling Couture. Aynsley knew right then and there that she'd been beat—at least in terms of presentation. They practically had a finished *Couture* layout, complete with photo shoot and text, written by Ava, of course. And honestly, listening to them talk about the marriage of high fashion and street style, even Aynsley thought it was a good idea. Essay plus fashion spread? Well, *that* was something that intellectually challenged *Style* magazine couldn't copy. Clearly Nadine and Ava had done their homework. But could they sell Isabel on Rocawear?

"Now, I know that *Couture* has a more European sensibility than most fashion magazines," Nadine explained. "And hip-hop is home-grown Americana. But that puts us in a unique position to really meld the two aesthetics in a more exciting way than anyone else has."

Isabel, Kiki, and Dieter stared at Nadine like she was from outer space. They were used to thinking the girl was a waste of oxygen, yet here she was, strutting her talents and blowing fresh air all over the place. Aynsley was actually proud.

"Who took these pictures?" Kiki demanded.

"I did," Nadine replied humbly.

"Hmm," Kiki replied. "Interesting. Isabel . . ."

"I am ready to deliberate," Isabel announced. "If you ladies will step outside."

Ava, Aynsley, and Nadine shuffled into the hallway, heaping congratulations on one another before falling into nervous silence. Not five minutes later, Kiki opened the door and ushered them back inside.

"My saviors," Isabel trilled. "*Je t'aime!* And this idea. The Bling Couture. I have been getting pressure from my advertisers to court the urban market, so it is *parfait*. *Brava!* And, Aynsley, nice talk," she added with a condescending smile.

Ava and Nadine hugged and then turned to hug Aynsley, too, with these annoyingly consoling looks on their faces.

"So," Kiki added. "What this means is that Nadine

and Ava's idea will run in the next issue. You two will be on hand to help style and shoot it. That's one of your prizes. But the real prize is that you lucky bitches get to spend the evening at our celebrity gift suite in the Pierre Hotel."

"We get a suite?" Nadine asked.

"Not just a suite," Aynsley interrupted. "A gift suite. It's the ultimate swag-fest. Companies stock plush hotel rooms with their hottest new toys and trinkets, and let A-listers come in and take whatever they want. The hope is that the celebs will use the new products, and then the rest of the world will want it all, too."

"And tonight, you'll be the celebrities," Kiki said.

"No flippin' way," Nadine exclaimed. "You mean we can take whatever we want—like Halloween candy?"

"*Exactement,*" Isabel said. "And just so you have something to bring it all back with, we have these for you." She handed over two Fendi Silver bags.

"The Fendi Silver. Nice," Aynsley said admiringly. She was on a waiting list to get one of her own.

"Did you say the suite thing is today?" Ava asked as she accepted her Fendi.

"*Oui.* So off with you now," Isabel said. "You and

Nadine are excused for the day, and you may come in late tomorrow as well. Have fun. And *merci* for the hard work. Now, if you'll excuse me, we have the accessories department due for their ideas meeting now."

As they gathered their stuff, Aynsley saw Ava whisper something into Nadine's ear. *"You can't be serious?"* Nadine said in response. "Can't you reschedule? Damn, how often do you get an opportunity like this?"

Ava looked miserable for someone who'd just won such a sweet prize. "I can't," she said. "I'm sorry."

"Hey, Sly," Nadine called. "Ava can't go to the Pierre. She's got some doctor's appointment in Long Island."

"Looks like I'll be your date then," Aynsley said, flashing a meaningful look at Nadine. All summer long, Ava had been disappearing for doctors' appointments. The other girls couldn't decide if she was seeing a shrink or what—but Aynsley wasn't about to press the issue now. Not with a suite full of exclusive swag awaiting her.

"I'm sorry, Nadine," Ava lamented. "But you'll have fun with Aynsley."

"Of course she will," Aynsley confirmed. "And I'll bring you some goodies, Ava," she added graciously.

Staffers were beginning to file past them into the

conference room. "Well, I'd better get going," Ava said. "At least I got my Fendi."

"Nice bag," said Marceline, the accessories editor as she breezed into the conference room. "And nice mention in *The Observer*, Ava," she added.

"What are you talking about?" Ava asked her.

"Hot off the presses," Marceline said, reaching into her Marc Jacobs tote. She pulled out the pink newspaper and opened to the party pages. There, on the bottom right was a picture of Ava with a handsome, older man whom Aynsley thought looked vaguely familiar.

"It's you and the Silver Fox!" Nadine exclaimed.

Ava looked like a deer caught in the headlights. "I've gotta go," she said, then she bolted down the hallway like her skirt was on fire.

Aynsley and Nadine looked more closely at the caption. It read: Couture*'s Ava Barton chats with Daniel Aames, executive editor at* Style.

Marceline shrugged. "Daniel's an old dog. He loves to get his picture taken with pretty young things. Though after *Style*'s latest shenanigans I doubt he'll be invited to any more *Couture* parties."

Aynsley looked at Nadine. Her eyes were narrowed in deep concentration. "What?" Aynsley asked. "So she got her picture in the paper." It wasn't a big deal; it happened to Aynsley all the time.

Nadine stayed silent a moment longer. Then she shook her head. "Let's worry about Ava later. Right now, we got ourselves some partying to do."

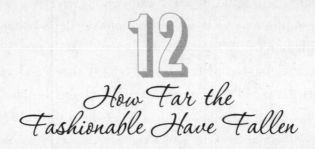

12

How Far the Fashionable Have Fallen

CALLIE COULD NOT REMEMBER ever feeling so tired in her entire life. Which was weird considering that she'd been in bed a whole day. Ever since the humiliation-fest that was her meeting with Kiki, Marceline, and Quinn, she'd done nothing but fester under the sheets in her dorm room. She'd refused to answer the door, knowing it was probably Ava on the other side. She refused to recount the details of that awful meeting while enduring Ava's selfless sympathy. Besides, Ava surely knew all the details of what Callie had done by now, via the office gossip mill.

Callie's one consolation was that Nadine had made

herself scarce, camping out at chez Rothwell. *Ugh*—she couldn't bear to think of the Rothwell town house without shuddering at the memory of Aynsley's bedroom inquisition.

Callie looked at her clock. It was three o'clock—she'd managed to skip both breakfast and lunch. She yanked on the Bexley High T-shirt she'd buried at the bottom of her drawer when she arrived in New York. What did it matter now if anyone else realized Bexley High wasn't some elite Midwestern prep academy? The charade was over. All of her charades were over. And Callie's life felt as good as over.

She extracted a brown banana and a bottle of flat Diet Coke from the fridge. Breakfast of champions, she joked to herself. She carried her meal back to her bed and cleared off the pile of *People* magazines that had been her sole company these past few days. She hadn't been able to read her beloved fashion magazines, nor had she checked out the Fashionista's daily dish. It was just too painful a reminder of all that she'd lost.

She pushed over the pile of magazines, knocking her cell phone to the floor. She worried that her parents, who hadn't heard from her since Tuesday, might have dispatched a search party by now, so she flipped open her cell and scrolled through her messages. Callie harbored vague hopes that Julian would have contacted her by now; the last she'd heard from him was a quick email saying he was off to the Hamptons. But all she had were six messages from Ava, two from her mom, and a couple from some friends at home. Nothing from Julian. Nothing from *Couture*. But Callie knew that Isabel was due back from Europe today, so she anticipated the impending *you're-fired* announcement any moment now.

The familiar chime of Callie's phone startled her and she glanced at the caller ID. Her heart skipped a beat. It was *Couture*. The moment of truth had arrived, and she suddenly felt sick to her stomach. She took a breath and answered.

"Hello," she said unsteadily.

"Hey, you're there!" Ava sounded relieved.

"Oh, yeah. Sorry I've been out of it."

"I know. I've been worried. You okay?"

How could Ava not know? Callie'd assumed that word of her disgrace was echoing through the hallways of *Couture*, with Aynsley shouting loudest of all. But maybe Aynsley hadn't deigned to take time out of her busy daily socialite schedule to spread the news.

"I think I've got some flu thing," Callie lied.

"Poor, baby," Ava said. "Isabel mentioned you're working on a special project for her, though. That's great, because, well—I've got a little bit of bad news for you—"

"What? What is it?" Callie asked. Had they made *Ava* the messenger to fire her?

"I feel weird telling you this because it's good news for me." Ava paused. "But Nadine and I won the contest. Our Bling Couture feature is going in the magazine."

"Oh," Callie said flatly. "Congratulations." She hadn't had much time to work on her *How Green Is Your Runway?* idea anyway—what with slaving away to keep Aynsley from blowing her prep-school cover and all. But Callie had left Aynsley her proposal, half hoping that the lazy diva would run with it and save both of their reputations at *Couture*.

"Thanks. But I liked your idea a lot," Ava replied. "I think, with a little more development time, you could really sell it."

"Thanks," Callie said, absently twisting her hair around her index finger until it throbbed. "So what was your big prize?"

"Oh, an evening at a celebrity gift suite at the Pierre," Ava explained.

"Fun," Callie replied, glad that she could *at least* be happy for Ava. "You'll rake in the goods."

"Actually . . . Aynsley will," Ava said mournfully. "I can't go. I've got a doctor's appointment."

"*What!?* I mean—you're just seeing an allergist, right? Can't you skip it?"

"Um. Well," Ava faltered. "It's just that, this doctor is really hard to get appointments with. And then I have this thing at my parents after, so I'm going straight to Port Jefferson."

"That sucks," Callie groaned, as if she were the one missing out. "I mean, it's not like Aynsley needs the free goodies, ya know?"

"I know. The last thing that girl needs is another pair of Manolos," Ava said ruefully.

Manolos? Manolos! With a jolt, Callie remembered her ginormous Visa bill. Two thousand six hundred and forty-three dollars. No amount of hiding under the covers was going to erase that massive balance. She gave Ava a rushed good-bye and snapped her flip phone closed.

After her talk with Ava, Callie was left feeling antsy. Here she was, stuck in limbo—her whole future as murky as the Hudson River. And, obviously, Kiki had made up some special-project lie to hide Callie's indiscretions at *Couture*. She took some deep yoga breaths to calm her ragged nerves, but it didn't work. She had a nagging urge to smoke a cigarette. Callie could have sworn she'd seen Nadine shove a pack of American Spirits into her lingerie drawer the other day.

When Callie walked over to Nadine's dresser, it was like opening Pandora's Box: lacy teddies, hair falls, jangly gold bracelets, and snatches of paper practically jumped out at her. Callie had to pull out half the crap as she hunted for the cigarettes. She was about to reload Nadine's junk when she did a double take: Why would Nadine have a picture of Julian in her lingerie drawer?

Callie took a closer look at the black-and-white print and gasped. There was Nadine, full-on kissing an amused-looking Julian, with her ample cleavage wrapped up in his seersucker blazer. Callie dropped the photo back into the drawer, as if it were covered in slime.

Normally, such a discovery would've inspired an epic Callie Ryan hissy fit. Normally, she'd have been on the phone to Ava immediately, bitching up a storm about Nadine's treachery. Then she'd have gone straight to Nadine, to give the little ho a piece of her mind. But in the midst of her fashion disgrace, Callie was too dispirited to even feel betrayed. In fact, she would have bet money that it was her total disregard for bad karma that had caused the treacherous hook-up in the first place.

Callie showered and got dressed in her favorite red-and-white Forever 21 cotton sundress and her Ipanema flip-flops. Then she went outside for the first time since Tuesday. The air was thick and wet, and the wind felt like somebody's hot breath choking down her neck. The streets were ripe with unpleasant city smells. *Amazing how things change,* Callie mused. *Last week these streets were lined with gold; today they're coated with garbage.*

Callie wandered aimlessly down Broadway, dodging happy couples and window-shopping hipsters. She cut east on to Astor Place, then found herself on St. Marks—the hangout of choice for the punked-out set. She thought back to a night a few weeks ago when she and Ava had come down here for drinks. Aynsley had taken them to some swanky bar earlier in the evening—those being the days when Aynsley and Callie pretended to tolerate each other—and Aynsley had sprung for cocktails and dinner at a posh hotspot. After Ava and Callie left Nadine and Aynsley at the Fire Opal Bar that night, they'd strolled through

Gramercy Park, fantasizing about their futures—Callie as a hot designer, Ava as a famous editor. Well, at least one of them was on her way.

Callie stopped in front of Roots, the dive bar where she and Ava had gone that night—the same spot where Callie had introduced Ava to a hottie named Reese. There was a sign in the bar's dingy window that practically called Callie's name: COCKTAIL WAITRESS NEEDED. MUST BE AT LEAST 18.

Sure, Callie was only sixteen, but when had she ever let a nagging little detail stop her? Besides, St. Marks was full of shops where she could score a new fake ID. Callie stepped into one of them. Ten minutes and $15 later, she was holding her new Minnesota driver's license: Michelle Smith, aged twenty-one—Capricorn.

License in hand, Callie walked back across the street and into Roots. Inside the bar, the air was dim and cool, smelling of old beer and peanuts.

"We're closed," said a gruff, tattooed bartender.

"Um, I'm here about the job," Callie replied.

"You ever waitress before?" the bartender queried.

"Uh-huh." This was partly true. Back in Ohio, she'd carried a heavy oval tray or two to help out a family friend with his catering business. How hard could serving beer be?

"And how old are you?" the bartender asked with a definite look of suspicion in his eyes.

"Twenty-one," Callie insisted.

He eyed her coyly. "Lemme see your ID, then."

As Callie passed over her newly minted license with steady hands, she wondered if maybe she'd missed her calling. She should have been an actress.

"What's the capital of Minnesota?" he barked.

"St. Paul," Callie replied without hesitation. For once, she was lucky to be a Midwesterner.

The bartender smirked. "Did your homework, huh? This looks hot off the presses. Where'd ya get it?" He handed it back to Callie and waved his beefy hands as if in surrender. "No, wait. Don't tell me. I don't wanna know. One of my girls quit and I'm understaffed. Can you start tonight?"

"Sure. Why not?" It wasn't like she had anything else going on.

"Okay. Come in at seven. We've got a pretty simple system here. We're a basic Budweiser kind of place."

"Got it," Callie said gratefully.

"I'll have a Roots T-shirt for you," he promised her. "And wear a short skirt. You'll get better tips."

Callie agreed. She walked out into the oppressive

early August afternoon. A week ago she'd been a celebrated fashion designer clad in couture. Now she was a cocktail waitress in a T-shirt and miniskirt. In the back of her mind, she heard Aynsley's snooty drawl whispering, *How far the fashionable have fallen*.

13

The Surreal Life

IT WAS QUITE CUTE, REALLY—seeing Nadine so beside herself. The minute they entered the Premiere Suite on the thirty-ninth floor of the Pierre Hotel, the girl practically started jumping up and down. Aynsley vaguely remembered doing the same one Christmas when she was five.

"Holy shit, I didn't believe places like this actually existed," Nadine exclaimed.

Aynsley understood how someone who'd never seen a gifting suite before could get so excited: the huge two-bedroom apartment in the swank Pierre Hotel had sweeping views of Central Park, and every surface in the place was covered with a glittering assortment of electronics, cosmetics, accessories, clothing, and more. All of it free for the taking. There was a buffet set up with champagne and strawberries, finger sandwiches and crudités. In one of the bedrooms there was a makeshift beauty station, manned by girls on hire from Bliss to give manis, pedis, and mini-facials. Aynsley guessed that to a neophyte like Nadine this suite must have felt like Candyland.

"Oh. My. God!" Nadine cried. "They're giving out laptops?" She ran to look at the computers, then was distracted by a display of high-end plaid messenger bags that looked totally tacky to Aynsley. "I don't get this, Sly," Nadine continued. "I mean, who gives away such expensive shit?"

Aynsley sighed. Sometimes Van Buren could be such a rube. "I already explained this to you. The manufacturers hire PR companies to lure celebrities into using their new products. In fact, if I'm not mistaken, this suite is hosted by your nemesis, Lucy Gelson." Lucy Gelson was the publicist who'd been in charge of the Cutting Edge Gala, and Nadine had been number one on Lucy's shit list—until the night of the gala itself, when Aynsley disappeared from the velvet rope and became shit-lister numero uno herself.

"Will she be here?" Nadine asked in a panic.

Aynsley smirked. "Who cares? We're *Couture*'s guests. The suite is ours for the night. She has to treat us like royalty no matter how much it burns her butt to do it. She'll kiss your ass like a pro, too. After all, event publicists are paid to lie."

As if on cue, the blond barracuda herself strolled in, lips as big as pufferfish, Botoxed eyes hidden under oversized black Gucci shades. "Darlings," Lucy cried, flipping back her platinum hair. "Isabel told me you'd be here. *So good* to see you."

Aynsley couldn't help but chuckle at the look of shock on Nadine's face as Lucy planted a kiss on each of her cheeks.

"We've had quite a day," Lucy gushed. "I don't want to name names but we've had two stars from *Gossip Girl*, and one from *Grey's Anatomy*, not to mention an eco-loving heartthrob, the pop star currently at number two on Billboard's Top 100, and the hottest celebrity family in the business. We're getting written up in the *Post*. And the Fashionista was here before."

"*Oh, really?* You know who she is?" Aynsley asked.

"I do," Lucy said, putting a finger over her swollen lips. "But I'm paid to be discreet."

"Well, then, how about a drink, Luce? Nadine and

I would like a little celebratory champagne," Aynsley noted, savoring the chance to boss the evil bitch around.

"Of course," Lucy replied, snapping her fingers at a waiter.

"And when is everyone clearing out?" Aynsley inquired, her voice as light as spun cotton. "We plan to have some people over to share the celebration."

A shadow crossed Lucy's face. "We should wrap up by six. Give you girls plenty of time to shop. Shall I call up for something to eat? They have the most divine strawberries."

"We'll have the deluxe sushi platter," Aynsley replied. "And fresh raspberries. That'll be all," she added imperiously.

As Lucy skittered away, Nadine stared at Aynsley, her mouth ajar. "What?" Aynsley asked.

"This is just beyond bizarre. Free booty. Lucy kissing *our* booties. I think I'm in heaven."

"Welcome to the surreal life of the rich and famous. Now let's get you shopping," Aynsley said.

She trailed Nadine around as her friend tried on silky lingerie that practically split from the force of her bosom, and a pair of bright red suede boots a half-size too big (Aynsley recommended insoles and thick socks). Then Nadine loaded up on some organic lavender body milk and picked up a handheld video player. The girl was racing around in a frenzy, as if any minute now, a giant hand was going to swoop down and take away all the swag. After a while, she looked up long enough to notice that Aynsley's bag was practically empty.

"What's the deal, Sly? Don't you want any of this stuff?"

"I spied some cute Oscar de la Renta heels that I'll take. And maybe one of those leather bracelets. But other than that, I'm good."

"How can you pass up a free laptop?"

"It's a PC. I'm a Mac-only kind of girl," she replied dismissively.

"Shit, that's like not stopping to pick up a twenty-dollar bill in the middle of the street."

Aynsley just shrugged. She wouldn't have taken cash off the street, either.

"They have a pedicure station in one of the bed-rooms," Aynsley said. "I'm going to get a quick foot job, then I'll meet you out here when the food is ready. And I'll make some calls—*you know*, rally the party people to join us. Any requests?"

"I already left a message for Sam," Nadine said somewhat shyly. "You think it'd be stupid to call Anezka and Zehna?"

"Not at all. Models love free stuff. And Lucy will be kissing your ass for real if they show," Aynsley replied. "Shall I call Hayden and Spencer? Are you still on with those guys?"

"I'm over them," Nadine said tersely. She was trying to hide it, but Aynsley could see that Nadine was over pretty much everyone who wasn't Sam Owens. Not that Aynsley could blame her; Sam was hot, successful, talented—and actually quite nice. If he *weren't* so nice, Aynsley might have craved him herself. "Just invite Jules and some people," Nadine added.

"I'm a little over Jules at the moment," Aynsley said.

"You and your brother in a spat?"

"Not really. Just a case of too much togetherness. It's time for him to go back to Europe," Aynsley replied. She found it strange that she resented Julian for his little Callie seduction. It wasn't as if she liked the little faker—although she *was* insanely curious about why Callie'd been MIA all week. She had some investigating to do. But, for now, her feet needed attention. She disappeared into the bedroom where, next to the black-and-white-tiled bathroom, a makeshift beauty station awaited her. She eyed the frilly surroundings; the place was decorated very much to Cecilia Rothwell's taste, all damask and floral, very European baroque. Aynsley so preferred the Soho Grand with its sleek modern decor and painfully hip staff.

By the time Aynsley's pedicure was done, she'd called a dozen of her friends about tonight's soiree. Once her toes were dry, she slipped on her tan-and-blue wood-heeled Nanette Lepore sandals and returned to the living room just in time for room-service sushi. As the waiter laid out the spread, Aynsley made sure Lucy and her minions got the message that it was time for them to pack up and clear out.

When it was just her and Nadine, Aynsley grabbed a fresh bottle of Dom Pérignon from the fridge and popped it open. She brought the bottle and two flutes over to her friend, who was sitting on a pink couch and looking dazed.

"You need another drink," Aynsley declared.

"Damn straight, I do." Nadine accepted the champagne.

"Here's to your reversal of fortune," Aynsley said, raising her glass.

"It *has* been quite the turnaround. What a difference a week makes," Nadine agreed. "My head's spinning."

"Not as much as it will be. Tonight we party like rock stars," Aynsley added.

"Amen to that," Nadine replied.

• • • • • • • • • • •

Two hours later, they'd gone through the sushi, the raspberries, a gooey slice of Valrhona chocolate cake, and another bottle of Dom. Aynsley checked the clock. Her posse would soon be arriving. She went to the wet bar and started mixing martinis while Nadine stared out at the skyline, which had turned a dusky purple.

At nine, the door chimed as Aynsley's friends, and friends of friends, began arriving en masse. One of her DJ pals showed up, bringing with him his portable sound kit. He plugged his iPod and turntable into speakers and played a heady mix of trip-hop. Aynsley directed a bunch of guys to lug the heavy oak dining table against the wall to make way for a dance floor. Then she kicked off her sandals and started grooving.

Soon, nearly everyone else in the suite had abandoned their drinks to boogie alongside Aynsley. The room was a swirl of skinny girls and muscular guys all clad in designer glam, all gyrating and grinding like they were headlining at the Pussycat Club. Nadine should have been front and center in this bacchanal, but Aynsley didn't spot her anywhere. She turned to hunt her down but was intercepted by Walker Graystone. *Ugh!* How'd he get in? Sometimes her circle of friends was way too incestuous. Walker sidled up to her with all the charm of an Italian gigolo.

"Hi, beautiful. Can I get you a drink?" he asked her.

"I'm the hostess here. I can fix my own," she replied.

"Want to do some lines, then?"

"So eighties. No thanks."

"At least let me refill your champagne."

"Fine," Aynsley replied. "But it will have to count as our last date—ever."

Walker smiled. "You know, Aynsley, I'm a guy. The more you reject me, the more I'm going to sniff around. It's in the DNA."

"So, following that logic, if I sleep with you right now, do you promise to go away?"

He laughed. "I might wind up bewitched. But still, it's worth a shot," he said with a leer.

"Please. *Hey, Natasha!*" Aynsley yelled to her absurdly beautiful chum from school. Natasha strode over, her sexy Slavic eyes looking intrigued. "This is Walker Graystone," Aynsley said, making a proper introduction.

"I know who he is," Natasha purred, batting her eyelashes.

"Why don't you two go have some fun together?" Aynsley suggested.

Walker laughed. "I hardly need a pimp," he said archly.

"But I'm just being a good hostess," Aynsley replied.

Walker eyed Natasha, who looked typically ravishing in a plunging D&G zebra-print dress and mile-high stilettos. "I see your point," he said gratefully. "Natasha, would you like to dance?"

"First vodka, then dancing," Natasha declared, leaving Aynsley with a wink as she led Walker away.

Aynsley continued her search for Nadine. Usually, the girl gravitated toward the spotlight like a magnet to metal. But Aynsley found her sitting in a bedroom with her pile of loot spread out on the Frette sheets. She was drinking a bottle of Evian.

"You're *hiding*? Drinking *Evian*? Time for an intervention. *What* is wrong, Van Buren?" Aynsley inquired.

"I'm fine. Having a great time," Nadine said unconvincingly.

"Please, you've never lied to me before. It's what I most adore about you. So spill it. What's up?" Aynsley said.

"I dunno. I guess I'd hoped Sam would show. He totally helped me out with my project and I wanted to thank him."

"You wanted to thank him, did you?" Aynsley asked with a smirk. "I can imagine the many ways you'd like to express your gratitude."

"Oh, yeah. I've got lots of ideas. But damn it, he's not even here."

"His loss, then," Aynsley replied. "Now, shall we put your goodies away and get back to the party? You cleaned up, I see."

"I got some stuff for Ava. And one thing for Callie—she'd be impossible to deal with otherwise, right?" Nadine complained. "And I got some great sunglasses and some hair products. Did you see they had LuxeLife StraightEdge here? I cannot believe Lucy is slinging that crap after it singed off my hair. Just wait until somebody like Naomi Campbell loses her locks to that shit—then we'll see who's laughing."

Aynsley smiled. Nadine's accident with LuxeLife's straightening treatment had left her deep in the *Couture* doghouse, a doghouse from which she'd *just* been released, thanks to Bling Couture.

"And there was all this great menswear stuff," Nadine added, "so I got a kidskin wallet and these crazy sunglasses."

"For Sam, I take it?"

"Gotta express my gratitude somehow. And if he doesn't want the stuff, I'm sure one of my Philly friends will."

Out in the living room, the DJ had switched to old

eighties tunes, and someone, it sounded like Walker, was rapping to Blondie's "Rapture." Roars of laughter and applause mingled with the clinking sound of glasses.

"Okay, enough with the moping. What you need is another drink. Champagne? Cosmo? One of those awful White Russians you like?"

"I'll just have a beer," Nadine said with a smile.

"Fine. But you better get chugging. It's not a real party until Nadine Van Buren takes her shirt off!"

"Screw you, Sly," Nadine said affectionately.

"Well, that depends entirely on how wasted I get now, doesn't it?" she said with a cheeky laugh. Then she grabbed Nadine's hand and led her back to the party.

14

The Scene of the Crime

AVA WAS BAFFLED. CALLIE had been MIA all week long, not showing for work—because of some top-secret project, according to Isabel. But then, Friday afternoon, out of the blue, the following text: *Must talk!! SuperUrgent!!! Meet me @ Roots 2nite. Drinks on me.* ☺ *Cal.*

Ava had no clue what was going on. Had Callie and Julian broken up? Had she and Aynsley blown up? Frankly, Ava had had enough angst this week without a big Callie emergency. Her meeting with Daniel had been worse than awful. Though he'd been as polite and smooth as ever, he'd also made it perfectly clear that he had no intention of letting Ava go without a fight. If she walked away, he'd threatened to drag her name through the mud, to announce to anyone who'd listen that the whole arrangement had been Ava's idea, and he'd merely been seduced into it. But if, on the other hand, Ava just kept her chin up and her mouth shut until the end of the summer, they could part amicably and "stay friends," he'd said with a devilish grin.

Still, Ava was glad to hear from Callie. It wasn't like she had anything else going on tonight. Her parents were up in Maine for two weeks, so there'd be no company at their house. Nadine and Aynsley had strolled into the *Couture* offices at two and, upon discovering that most of the staff had left at noon to get a jump on the weekend, they'd jetted right back out again— apparently in need of rejuvenating spa treatments after Wednesday night's celebrity suite soiree. An event, Ava noted bitterly, that *she* should've been at, instead of stuck at the Four Seasons with Daniel.

Ava took a deep breath. She didn't mean to be bitchy. It wasn't Nadine or Aynsley's fault that she'd missed out on the Pierre. And Nadine had, at least, collected a grab bag of swag on her behalf, including a silky lingerie set, a L.A.M.B. watch, and an MP3 player. And she, of course, would always have her Fendi Silver.

Ava glanced at her new watch. It was past eight and

the offices were eerily empty. She finished typing up the rest of her notes for Bling Couture before shutting down her computer and catching the R train downtown. It was only when she got off at 8th Street that she realized Callie hadn't told her when to meet her. Oh, well. She was here now. And she could definitely use a beer.

Roots was still quiet; the after-work drinkers were wrapping up happy hour and the weekend partiers had yet to arrive. Ava stood in the doorway, allowing her eyes to adjust to the dim light as she scanned the place for Callie. Not seeing her, she plunked down at a corner table, wiping her sweaty hands on her Bitten jeans and adjusting the strap of her Chloé kimono top. She pulled out a copy of *Vanity Fair* to read the article about Hillary Clinton that everyone at *Couture* had been buzzing about.

"Don't you know, reading in the dark will ruin your eyes?"

The voice sounded like Callie, but when Ava looked up it was a cocktail waitress in front of her. It took her a full second to realize that Callie *was* the cocktail waitress.

"Cal—*hi*. What's going on? You working here now?" For a moment Ava wondered if this was Callie's secret *Couture* assignment, going undercover as a cocktail waitress.

Callie sighed dramatically and slumped into the chair opposite Ava. "Butch, I'm taking my break now," she called to the tattooed bartender. Then she turned to Ava. "I've got a half hour. That's when things pick up here."

"So this is where you've been hiding all week?" Ava asked.

"Sort of. I started yesterday. I work nights."

"I don't get it," Ava said. "Then why haven't you been in the office? What's your big secret assignment?"

Callie's hazel eyes blazed with disbelief. "Don't tell me they haven't told you?"

"Only that you're working on some project from home—"

"Yeah, like my résumé," Callie retorted. She shook her head, sending her dirty-blond ponytail lashing against her face. "I'm pretty much fired. I'm sure the only reason they haven't fully axed me yet is that they're too busy with the new issue."

"Stop," Ava demanded. "Get me an appletini. And then back up to the beginning and tell me *exactly* what's going on."

"Oh, yeah, drinks. Some waitress I am." Callie jumped up and went to the bar before returning with Ava's green cocktail and launching into her week: the meeting with Quinn, Marceline, and Kiki; the suspension; the Visa bill; her week-long pity party; and the new job.

"Oh, and while I'm sharing, I don't really go to a prep school," Callie admitted bashfully. "I lied about that, too. So, I'm not a private-school girl. And I'm not a designer, either."

Ava stared at Callie. She knew her friend was trying to be flip, but she could see how bad she was hurting. She felt really bad for her. And it didn't seem fair, either. As far as Ava was concerned, Callie's lies, while unwise, were small-fry and insignificant compared to her own.

"You're *still* a designer," Ava said earnestly. "You've got talent. There's no faking that. And no matter what happens at *Couture*, no one can take that away."

Callie shrugged and attempted a melancholy smile. "Well, you know what they say, if a tree falls in the forest and no one hears it, does it make a sound? Well, if a fashion designer designs but *Couture* has blacklisted her, does she even matter?"

"Yes, you do," Ava said adamantly.

"It's nice of you to say, but it's just because you're so naïve."

For a second, Ava felt a flash of anger, followed by a

slap of shame. She wasn't nearly as naïve as Callie thought she was, though once again, this was no time to bring up her own travails.

"Oh, and to top off my beautiful life, Julian hasn't called," Callie added, looking utterly defeated.

"Yeah, but that's typical of him, no?" Ava asked. "He's always in and out of town."

Callie rolled her eyes. "In and out of every*thing* and every*one* from the looks of it. I also found a picture in Nadine's drawer—of Julian and Nadine *totally* kissing."

Ava shrugged, unsure of what to say. She didn't know a lot about guys, but Julian didn't strike her as the monogamous type. Frankly, the kiss with Nadine didn't surprise her much, either.

"I know Jules gets around," Callie said, as if reading Ava's mind, "but things were just starting to heat up between the two of us. I really thought he was falling for me. But then Aynsley had to butt her bitchy nose in. I just know that she's feeding him all kinds of lies about me, painting me as some power-hungry vixen. *I'm not!*" Callie cried. "You know how I am. He just needs to hear my side of the story."

"So tell him," Ava suggested. She looked around. The bar was starting to fill up with NYU students, and the East Village arty crowd had arrived, dressed in varying degrees of black, accessorized with piercings and tattoos.

"Yeah, maybe. If I ever get a hold of him." Callie looked around the bar, seeming to notice the sudden rush. "I'd better go before Butch yells at me. Can you believe he's actually named Butch? But he's not so bad. At least what you see is what you get, unlike all the backstabbers at *Couture*." Callie glanced at Ava's untouched cocktail. "You enjoy your drink. I'll check on you in a bit. Maybe I can get another break in a while and we can talk about you. I feel like I've been all blab-blab-blabbing about me."

"Okay, that'd be good," Ava said weakly, though there was no way she was going to tell Callie all about her. She'd wanted to last week. But that was back when she thought she had everything figured out. Now, Ava understood, she hadn't had a clue. Not at the beginning of the summer, when she first got involved with Daniel. And not at the Cutting Edge Gala, when she thought she'd ended it with Daniel. Now she was more muddled than ever, stuck in a quagmire.

She sat there, watching all the people in the bar. They were laughing, dancing, flirting, making out—all things you were supposed to do at twenty-one. She nursed her drink and watched Callie. Even as a waitress, she was good, subtly flirting with the guys, making the girls feel pretty and smart. The way she dashed back and forth swinging her tray around, you'd think she was a seasoned pro.

Ava had had enough of playing the wallflower. She looked for Callie to settle her tab and say good-bye but couldn't spot her. When she finally did, Callie was deep in conversation with some guy at the bar. By the way she was wildly gesticulating and totally missing Ava's attempts to say good-bye, it looked like a pretty important conversation. Ava fished a ten-dollar bill out of her bag and tried to slip it into the pocket of Callie's skirt. Then she realized—too late to escape—who Callie was talking to.

"Can you believe it? *Reese* is here," Callie exclaimed. "I've been telling him it's kismet that you're here, too, and trying to get him to come say hi—but I guess he's shy. Have you two even seen each other since the big date?"

Ava felt her face turn crimson.

"Our big date?" Reese inquired.

"Didn't she look amazing in that dress?" Callie gushed.

Ava stared at her Kenneth Cole slingbacks while Callie gabbed on, asking Reese where he'd taken Ava and where they'd be going next. Ava waited for Reese to tell Callie that he, in fact, had not set eyes on Ava since they'd first met here a month ago. In a way, Ava wished Reese would say *something*. Maybe then she'd be *forced* to tell Callie what had been going on with Daniel all summer.

But Reese didn't say a word. Ava sneaked a nanosecond of a glance at him while Callie prattled on. He was just as adorable as she remembered: the floppy blond hair, the gray-blue eyes, the funky-yet-traditional style. This evening's ensemble included skinny Duckie Brown cuffed trousers, a vintage *Speed Racer* T-shirt, and bowling shoes. Reese turned his head and caught Ava staring at him, a pained smile on his face. She quickly looked away.

"You two stay here and catch up. I'm gonna go get you a pitcher of beer—*on the house*," Callie said, flitting away.

"Well, well," Reese said in that adorable Kentucky drawl of his. "Returning to the scene of the crime."

"Um, I guess so," Ava stuttered. What she really wanted to say was "I'm sorry," but she was afraid of the can of worms that those two words might open.

"Just like black widows. And serial killers," Reese said lightly, though Ava felt the sting of his words.

"I've been busy," Ava said, realizing how lame the ubiquitous excuse sounded.

"Apparently so. All dressed up and going on dates. Too bad I can't remember ours."

"I've been busy *at work*," Ava exclaimed. She meant it as clarification, but it came out sounding bitchy and cold.

"Oh, so you've been busy?" Reese drawled. "Me, not so much. Just working fifteen-hour days on this documentary."

"I—I didn't mean that you weren't," Ava said. God, she was sucking at this. She couldn't flirt with guys, and she couldn't defend herself with them, either.

"Here's your beer," Callie said, delivering a frothy pitcher and two glasses with a flourish. "Sam Adams, the good stuff for the lovebirds."

"Why thank you, Miss Callie," Reese said, doling out his charm, which made Ava feel even worse. There'd be no cute Southern gallantries for her this time around.

Reese poured himself a glass of beer and then one for Ava. She glanced at him from lowered eyes as he drank half of it. He set his glass down and fixed his gaze on her. She felt like she was going to melt.

"Here's the thing I don't understand," Reese began,

speaking slowly, as if carefully choosing his words. "If I recall, it was you and your friend who came up to me at this bar a while back. Now, I plead guilty for emailing you, but if memory serves, you did answer back, even if you were a mite coy about getting together. But eventually, lo and behold, the lady says yes to coffee. And then never shows. Now, I don't know if that's a New York City thing, but where I come from, that is plain rude."

Ava didn't know what to say. Reese was 100 percent right on, and she had nothing to excuse her behavior. She never should've responded to Reese's emails, never should've said yes to a date, never should've gotten involved with Daniel. She wished she could erase it all, could rewind to the start of the summer and choose an entirely different path. But she couldn't. And contemplating that, and looking at Reese, trying to hide his hurt, she felt unbearably sad.

"*I'm sorry,*" she whispered just before the tears came. Then she jumped up from the table and ran out of the bar, leaving a stunned Reese in her wake.

15
Scavengers

CALLIE FELT LIKE HER ENTIRE body was coated in a film of beer. She'd worked from seven p.m. until four a.m. both Friday and Saturday night, then come home, only to sleep all day before returning to the bar again. She'd never been so exhausted in her life. But, she'd earned more than $450 in tips this weekend alone, which meant, in a few more weeks, she'd have her Visa bill covered. Still, she was relieved when, on Sunday night at nine, Butch sent her home, telling her not to return until Thursday night, when things heated up again.

Callie's sneakers squished with beer as she wove

through the throngs of punks and dreadlocked Rasta guys on St. Marks Place, cutting up Fourth Avenue to her dorm. That she'd barely had a chance to think about anything this weekend—not Julian or Nadine or *Couture*—was a major benefit of her hectic job. And it had been fun to bump into Reese, though she had no idea why Ava had ditched him. The poor sap looked so sad and stunned, left alone with his pitcher of beer. *Something* was going on with Ava, and Callie had to find out what. But first, she had another enigma to solve: Julian. Tonight, she planned to take Ava's advice and tell him her side of the story.

Callie was annoyed to find Nadine back at the dorm. She hadn't seen her all weekend long, but now she was sitting on her bed, wearing a pair of sweats, watching a DVD about Andy Warhol on her new laptop. Without stopping to chat, Callie breezed by her roommate, jumped into the shower, and rinsed off the beer stench. Stepping out, she slathered on some fancy lavender body lotion that Nadine had left out, and gooped some Paul Mitchell RoundTrip into her hair, letting it dry naturally in waves. She dusted on some Stila bronzing powder and Prada nude lip gloss and spritzed a bit of Chanel on her cleavage. Then she picked out her sexiest dress, a mermaid-fit copper Tahari number with slits up the thighs that she'd picked up for $50 at a second-hand shop, and slid it on—sans bra and with her sexiest La Perlas underneath.

"You look nice," Nadine said. "Big date?"

"Something like that," Callie said coldly.

"You done with the bathroom? I gotta pee."

"Be my guest," Callie replied. As soon as she heard the bathroom door click, she quickly went to Nadine's drawer, grabbed the picture of her and Julian, and plunked it into one of the silk-screen satchels she'd made. Then she slipped into her copper wedge platforms and was out the door.

Julian was at home tonight. This much Callie knew because he'd finally responded to one of her texts with a voice mail. He'd apologized about not being in touch. He'd lost his phone—or so he claimed. He'd also been out of town. Now he was zonked and was planning a quiet night in. He'd ended the message with a "miss ya, babe," a sign-off that had given Callie the courage to do what she was now about to do.

But standing in front of the imposing Rothwell brownstone, its second-floor lights blazing, Callie's courage was draining. Maybe Aynsley hadn't told him anything. Maybe she shouldn't confront him about Nadine. Maybe she should just go in there and act like nothing had ever happened. She was just his girlfriend, popping by for a little visit.

She rang the bell. No one answered. She rang it again. Finally, after the third try, she heard footsteps and then Julian appeared. He looked sleepy. He was shirtless and wearing a pair of khaki Nicole Farhi cargo pants.

"Oh, did I wake you?" Callie asked. She recalled Julian claiming he was tired, but she'd never known the guy to go to bed before two a.m.

He shook his head. "No. I was just reading the *Times* and must have dozed off."

Callie waited for Julian to invite her in, but instead he just stood at the door, looking perplexed. She cocked her head to the side and ever-so-slightly jutted out her cleavage. "What's a girl gotta do to get a drink around here?" she asked, licking her lips.

Julian shrugged. He turned around, leaving the door ajar. It wasn't the most hospitable invitation, but Callie followed him in, trailing him to the kitchen.

"What do you want?" Julian asked. "Water? Coke? Juice?"

Callie wondered what had happened to *champagne and strawberries*. "How about some wine?" she asked.

"I think we've got some white open," Julian said,

reaching into the fridge for a bottle of Chardonnay. He poured Callie a glass and got himself an Amstel. He sat down at the dining room table and Callie positioned herself on the edge of his chair.

"Be careful," he warned her. "This is a Chippendale. Very expensive."

"Oh, sorry," Callie said. She pulled up a chair next to Julian, slid off her sandal, and ran her bare foot up his leg. "So, have you missed me?" Callie cooed.

"Yeah. 'Course," Julian said. "But I've just been blasted with all this stuff to do. My lease fell through for my apartment in Providence, so I had to find a new place before term starts in a few weeks. And I've got to make one more trip to Europe before summer's end."

"Well, it's a good thing I caught you on a quiet Sunday night," Callie said. She slid off her chair and grabbed Julian's hand. "Let's go sit on the couch."

Julian reluctantly followed her to the living room and sat down on a chintz-covered loveseat. "Now this is more comfy, isn't it?" Callie asked, nibbling Julian's neck.

Julian closed his eyes as Callie kissed him on the neck and ear, but when she came to his lips, they were cold and unresponsive. Somehow, his refusal to kiss her back was as humiliating as anything else that had happened this past week.

"What's wrong?" Callie cried.

"Nothing, babe. I told you. I'm exhausted."

"Too tired for this?" Callie asked, sliding her hand down the front of his cargo pants.

Julian grabbed Callie's wrist and removed it. "I told you, Cal. I'm beat."

"Guys are never too tired for sex. *What's going on?* Is it Nadine?"

Julian arched his green eyes in contempt. "What does Nadine have to do with anything?"

"I don't know. You tell me," Callie said, pulling the incriminating photo out of her bag. "You're the one who made out with her."

Julian eyed the photo impassively before flinging it onto the table. "That was just some party, when she was drunk as usual. Look, Callie. I don't have time for this right now."

It was then that Callie knew for sure that Aynsley had talked to Julian. How else to explain the sudden chill, his not calling, his not wanting her?

"I know why you're acting this way!" Callie accused.

"I'm not acting *any* way," Julian replied wearily. "I've explained to you a hundred times that I'm tired."

"*Bullshit*. I know what you've heard, and you know what? I'm going to tell you the whole truth." Callie could hear the desperation in her voice, but she had to do something to get through to Julian, to show him the real her. Whatever this problem was between the two of them, it was all just a big misunderstanding. He'd gotten the wrong idea about her. If he only knew the truth, he'd want to be with her. He'd be in love with her.

"I don't know if this is a good idea. Or the right time. Why don't we just get together later?" Julian asked.

"No. This is the right time!" Callie shouted. "It's time you knew the real me. My name is Callie Ryan. I'm seventeen years old. I live in Columbus, Ohio—where I go to Bexley High, which isn't a fancy private school like Dalton but just a regular old public school. I've never gone to a prep school. Or a boarding school. I don't summer in Europe. I've never even left the United States. I don't have a trust fund. My family doesn't own any expensive paintings. In fact, we don't have any original paintings at all. Just prints. We live in a regular house. It's a totally boring existence. The only thing that gets me excited at home is fashion. And all I've ever wanted to do in my entire life is be a fashion designer. And now that might not happen because when you and I went on our date in Williamsburg, I bought some silk screens from an artist and made some handbags out of them and before I knew what was happening the editors at *Couture* were going bat-shit over them and they assumed I made them. And I didn't tell them otherwise. I took credit for those silk screens even though someone else made them. And then those silk-screen bags got chosen for the Cutting Edge issue. And I was invited to the gala, which was beyond my wildest dreams. But I didn't have anything to wear to the damn thing, so I had to go into major debt to buy a gown. And now I owe like two thousand bucks on my credit card and have to be a cocktail waitress to pay it off. Which is fine because I don't have my internship at *Couture* anymore. The guy who made the silk screens found out about my bags and we had to go to the editors and tell them the truth and I'm on suspension, probably soon to be fired. Which will be the end of my career." Callie's voice caught on a sob, but she swallowed it, summoned her strength, and continued. "So that's the whole sordid story. Now you know. The real me."

Callie looked up at Julian's face, expecting some reaction: sympathy, horror, disgust. But he just looked mildly uncomfortable, as if he were trapped in a room with his drunk aunt Frances. Finally, he spoke.

"It sounds like you've got some heavy stuff going on in your life right now," he said. "Maybe we should cool off while you figure things out."

"I don't want to cool off. I need the people I care about around me right now."

"That sounds like a good idea, but Callie—I'm not your boyfriend. We had our fun, but now it's best if we have some time apart. In fact, I'm just gonna grab a shirt and my shoes and get out of here."

Before Callie had a chance to argue, Julian had slipped on his Prada flip-flops and a T-shirt and was at the front door. "You can let yourself out," he said, with a guilty lopsided grin. "I'll talk to you soon."

Callie sat there alone in the living room, utterly stunned. She'd been dumped before, but never so thoroughly humiliated. She slumped into her chair, cradling her head in her hands, and waited for the tears to come. But before they did, she heard the sound of heels clicking down the marble hallway. And just when she thought this night couldn't get any worse, there was Aynsley Rothwell standing at the entrance to the living room.

Callie just shook her head. "Oh, great. And I suppose you heard all of that."

Aynsley nodded her head. For once, that annoying

smirk of hers was missing. She walked slowly into the room, kicked off her heels, and sat on the chaise lounge opposite Callie.

"What are you waiting for?" Callie sneered. "Go ahead and laugh. You found me out. And now your brother knows everything, too. So the two of you can have a nice chuckle at my expense. And Nadine, too. The three of you can throw a Callie-flames-out party," Callie said, gesturing toward the discarded photo.

Aynsley picked up the photo, examined it, and placed it on the coffee table. "I *took* this picture, you know," she said.

"What for, to torture me?"

Aynsley shook her head. "More to show Nadine how ridiculous she gets when she's drunk. I take it she didn't get the message though," Aynsley said with an affectionate smile. "Anyhow, nothing happened between Jules and her, although I wouldn't put it past him. He's a total player."

"I'm beginning to see that," Callie said.

"He's like most guys. Once you sleep with them, the chase is over, and they can't wait to be miles away." Aynsley eyed Callie's wineglass. "If we're talking men, I think we need something stronger. I'm going to mix up some martinis. Care for one?"

Callie stared at Aynsley, trying to read her for signs of bitchiness, but she was already at the bar, pulling out the Ketel One. "Okay. I guess so," Callie said.

"Good. I mix a mean 'tini." Callie watched as Aynsley expertly measured, iced, shook, and strained the cocktails, poured them into delicate martini glasses, and garnished each one with an olive. "Here you go," Aynsley said, handing her the drink. "Enjoy. And please don't cry over Jules. He's not worth your tears. Trust me, you're not the first friend of mine he's done this to."

Callie did a double take. Had Aynsley just referred to her as a friend? "So—so you didn't tell him about me?" Callie asked incredulously.

"Of course not. Besides, what's to tell? That you fibbed about your private school? That was foolish, but people in Manhattan lie all the time. It's one of my pet peeves about this town. As for that other stuff with the bag, well, that's unfortunate because those silk-screen purses are really pretty amazing."

"Too bad they're not mine."

Aynsley narrowed her brown eyes. "Of course they are. You shouldn't have lied about the fabric, but Kiki is being a bit of a hypocrite about all of this. Fashion designers are scavengers by nature, relying on other people's ideas, fabrics, colors for inspiration. If you're going to be a designer, you should get comfortable with that."

"It's funny you say that. I'm always drawing inspiration from all kinds of things—old movies, paint colors, decor magazines—but I've always felt guilty about it. Like I'm stealing or something."

"I'm sure most young designers feel that way," Aynsley replied, twirling the olive in her drink. "But even when they feed off other people's ideas, they transform them into marvelous and totally new things."

"I never thought of it like that," Callie said with a tentative smile.

"Nothing to do but be honest about it," Aynsley said, raising her eyebrow at Callie. "Best to be honest in general. Own your weaknesses and all that crap."

"I guess so," Callie replied bashfully. "Though you're pretty much the last person in the world I thought I'd be honest with."

A broad smile stretched across Aynsley's angular face. "Now that's one of the most refreshing things I've ever heard you say," she said, laughing. "Come on now, let's have another drink. We have some getting acquainted to do."

"I am a diamond cluster hustler. Queen bitch, supreme bitch." —Lil' Kim

Filed under: Fashionista > Style

The Fashionista, as you know, is all about experimentation. I applaud those skinny little <u>Olsen twins</u> for bringing it with their quirky, oversized, ethereal style and creating a new look—<u>Boho chic</u>—only to jettison that same look when they launched their sophisticated new line, <u>Row</u>. The Fashionista even appreciates emulation, when it's done correctly. <u>Christina Aguilera</u>, for instance, has both copied and reinvented the siren style of the 1940s. It's certainly a welcome change from the barrage of <u>prostitute chic</u> that most young pop stars seem to favor.

But everything has its limits. It's not like the »

Fashionista to mock—okay, *maybe a little bit*. But when a *Couture* wannabe staffer parades around in a microskirted plaid suit that looks like my grandmother's couch, and then over-the-tops it with an I'm-so-ethnic African turban, well, it's time to phone the <u>fashion police</u>—and I'm just the girl to make that call. I mean, honey, you might think you're as bootylicious as <u>Beyoncé</u>, but to the rest of the world, you're looking like a pre-prison <u>Lil' Kim</u>: nothing but a crass and tacky diamond cluster hustler.

The Fashionista doesn't mean to be a *supreme* bitch, but as your friend in fashion, it's my duty to tell the whole truth and nothing but. And I know anyone brave enough to wear tummy chains can take the truth—even when it hurts.

Your faithful Fashionista

16
Little Miss Nobody

IT WAS RECKONING DAY. That's what Nadine told herself as she pulled her butt out of bed and tiptoed by a passed-out Callie who, it should be noted, smelled like a friggin' brewery. For some strange reason, Nadine prided herself on not being hungover this Monday morning. In fact, she hadn't been hungover all weekend, having maintained a mellow buzz at the gift suite and during Saturday night's club crawl with Aynsley. And she hadn't gone out last night at all, unlike the stinky snoring girl in the bed next to hers.

Nadine was glad to have a clear, ache-free head this morning. Because it was time to confront Ava, who'd been bullshitting Nadine, and the rest of them, all summer long. *Innocent virgin?* Yeah, and Nadine was a white girl from Wyoming. Ava was having an affair with that guy from *Style* magazine. Nadine had seen them together, photographed them having a lovers' spat, and on Friday, she'd uncovered the ultimate piece of proof: a picture of them together at the *Couture* gala published in a newspaper, no less.

It wasn't that she planned to go all moral on Ava for sleeping with a married guy old enough to be her dad. If Ava could snag a Silver Fox like that, Nadine would be the first to give her props. But it was the whole charade that pissed Nadine off. Miss Ava Barton had lied straight to Nadine's face, and nobody played Nadine Van Buren for a fool.

After showering, she grabbed her favorite kelly-green Bebe microminidress, the one that showed every one of Nadine's many curves, and then laced her black espadrilles all the way up her legs. It was her favorite bringing-sexy-back outfit, and it was for Sam's benefit. She was still a little stung that he hadn't shown up at the Pierre on Wednesday, so she decided that the least she could do was shine a spotlight on just what the man was missing. She put on her blond Afro wig, some purplish lipstick, and her stick-on eyelashes. Then she grabbed the photos of Ava and her man, a copy of *The Observer,* and was out the door.

She was in high spirits as she entered Conrad Media's gleaming office tower. She felt like a tigress about to trap her prey. Never mind that she actually *liked* her prey. Hey, lions probably didn't inherently dislike zebras, either, but nature was nature, right? And Nadine's nature was to seek the truth.

As she walked through *Couture*'s hallways, dodging rolling racks of Alice Roi, Abaeté, and Rodarte, she couldn't help noticing that every staffer's head swiveled as she walked by. Admiring her outfit, no doubt. Or taking a second look at the girl they'd all labeled with a giant L for Loser—*until last week* when she'd won the features contest.

As she walked by Kiki's office, Kiki, Dieter, and Marceline—looking like a funeral trio all dressed head-to-toe in black—were gathered around Kiki's computer, their eyes illuminated by the glow of the monitor.

"And speak of the devil," Dieter said in his guttural German accent as Nadine walked by.

"I know," Kiki trilled. "Though I'm a little jealous. I haven't been mentioned by the Fashionista. First Ava gets that glowy hit from the gala. And *now* Nadine."

"Would you *want* a mention like this?" Marceline

asked, talking about Nadine as if she weren't there.

"What are you guys talking about?" Nadine demanded. She could feel her warm, fuzzy mood starting to cool.

Kiki beckoned her in. "Scoot over, Dieter," she said before turning to Nadine. "It appears that you have been stung by the Fashionista."

"Huh?"

"Take a look."

Nadine looked at the monitor, where the latest Fashionista blog dominated the screen. She knew that Callie and Ava read the blog religiously, as did most of the fashion industry, but Nadine had missed the last couple of entries.

"*So?* It's a blog. BFD."

"It's a blog about *you*," Marceline crowed.

"My name is mentioned?"

"Just read."

Nadine dropped her bag and sat down in front of Kiki's computer. She couldn't believe her eyes. The outfit described was hers, but how could someone write this about her? It had to be a mistake.

"This . . . this is about *me?*" Nadine asked.

"Was there someone else wearing a plaid suit here on Wednesday?" Dieter asked before hiccupping out what sounded like a laugh. Nadine hadn't witnessed the man smile, much less laugh, all summer long.

"I wonder if this means the Fashionista is on staff," Marceline mused.

"Possibly," Kiki answered. "But Nadine was at the gift suite the other night in that getup, and she probably ran into half of Manhattan."

Nadine suddenly remembered Lucy saying that the Fashionista had been at the Pierre on Wednesday, too.

"Maybe Lucy Gelson is the Fashionista," Dieter clucked, before letting loose a new round of barking chuckles.

"Right," said Kiki. "And I'm Mother Superior."

Nadine felt like she'd been socked in the gut. She grabbed her bag, and, without a word of explanation, stormed out of the office and down the hall. There was no way she was gonna cry in front of those stuck-up fashion whores. She hoped the intern room would be empty, but when Nadine rounded the corner, Ava was already there, in front of her computer. Judging by the look of pity on her face, Nadine could tell she'd already read the Fashionista blog, along with the rest of New York's style elite.

"Nadine, *are you okay?*" Ava asked, her face full of concern.

"Yeah. I'm peachy fuckin' keen," Nadine retorted before turning on her heel and making a dash for the elevators.

"Nadine. Wait! Hold up," Ava called, jogging behind her.

Nadine violently punched the elevator button, wanting to be anywhere but at *Couture*. When the doors opened, Ava followed her inside. As they entered the lobby, Ava grabbed Nadine by the wrist and led her out the door the way a mother leads a crying child. "Come on. Let's go sit in Bryant Park for a bit," she said gently. "Give you time to get it together."

"I'm fine," Nadine said. She was better now. The shock had passed. Now she was just pissed at that Fashionista bitch for humiliating her.

"That outfit was totally part of our presentation. Isabel *got* that. She even commented on your ensemble," Ava said. "So the Fashionista is the clueless one."

"Easy for you to say. She said *nice* things about you!"

"It doesn't matter. I think it's an honor to be mentioned. It shows that you've hit a fashion nerve, like Paris or Lindsay."

"You mean like drunk drivers and coke addicts?" Nadine asked, aghast.

"I mean like famous people," Ava replied. "I felt

famous when she singled me out."

Nadine hadn't thought of it that way. Maybe this was the price of fame. They walked down 42nd Street to Crumbs, where Ava bought them a cupcake each and coffees. They crossed over to the park, sitting down at a small wrought-iron table.

"Feel better now?" Ava said between mouthfuls of mocha cake.

"Definitely," Nadine said, licking the chocolate from her fingers. "Cupcakes cure any woe."

After they'd finished their treats, Nadine felt calmer, and she also realized that this was the perfect opportunity to confront Ava about her affair. But unlike earlier this morning, she no longer felt like a lion about to tackle her prey. Ava had shown she was a true friend time and time again. But deep down, Nadine had the sense that by outing Ava, she'd somehow be doing her a favor.

"Ava, can I ask you something?" Nadine asked

"Ask me anything," Ava replied.

"What's up with you and Daniel Aames?"

Nadine watched Ava flush a pink as deep as the shade of the asymmetrical Jil Sander blouse she was wearing. "You did say ask you *anything*," Nadine gently prodded. "You're having an affair, aren't you?"

Ava's face went slack-jawed and blank.

"I mean, first I see you guys canoodling at Palais," Nadine continued. "And you were in the paper together. And I also saw you another time. In front of Bergdorf's, *arguing*. I even took a picture of it."

Ava opened her mouth to explain, but all that came out was a peal of laughter. She was laughing so hard, tears were streaming down her face, glistening in the pockets of her dimples. "Me and Daniel? An affair!" Ava gasped, before collapsing into a fit of giggles.

"Well, it did seem unlikely to me," Nadine began. "But the evidence is just too strong to ignore."

"Well, the evidence is wrong. *All* wrong," Ava insisted.

"If you're not sleeping with this guy, then what's the deal?" Nadine pressed on. She knew *something* had been going on and she had to finally know *what* that was.

"I met Daniel Aames at *Style* magazine, where I've been working as an editorial assistant for the last year," Ava began.

"What are you talking about? You work at *Couture*," Nadine corrected her. "And you just graduated from Vassar."

"No, I didn't. I graduated a year early, last spring, when I was twenty. I got the position at *Style* right after and I was so excited to finally be working in the fashion industry, but I was really more like Daniel's slave, not even a secretary or a personal assistant. I picked up his dry cleaning, hired tutors for his kids, set up his weekly manicure appointments. *Yes*—the man gets manicures."

"I'm not surprised," Nadine said wryly. "He looks like a dandy."

"A dandy and a smooth operator," Ava confirmed. "For the first nine months, he barely looked at me. I didn't even get *near* any editorial copy, never went to any fashion shoots, or any of that. The editors all treated me like shit, like I was some sort of bargain-basement reject, even though I worked my ass off twelve hours a day. So, I decided to quit, do something else, until one day, I'm looking at Vassar's job boards and I see the listing for the *Couture* internship. I applied, fibbed about my graduation date, and neglected to mention my *Style* job. I figured it was a long shot, and if I *did* get it, I could maybe write a big piece on my experiences at the two magazines. Anyhow, I didn't even think I'd be chosen, and when I was, I marched into Daniel's office and gave my notice."

"And then what?" Nadine asked.

"Don't worry. I'm getting to that," Ava replied with a rueful smile. "As soon as I told Daniel I was leaving to work at *Couture*, it was like Jekyll and Hyde. All of a sudden, he turned his charm on me. And when he wants to, that man has *a lot* of charm. He told me that he'd been watching me, testing me, which was why he'd been so cold: It had been part of a whole hazing strategy to see if I could cut it. He said that he'd been lobbying the *Style* editor in chief to make me a staff writer. And I was like, 'Oh, if you're countering with a new job, I guess I could reconsider.'"

"Well, the next thing you know, I'm promoted. The catch was that my first assignment was to do the *Couture* internship as an undercover spy."

"*Holy shit!* You're the mole!" Nadine exclaimed. She'd never even suspected Ava. In fact, Ava was the only one she hadn't been suspicious of. Clearly, she'd had *everything* wrong where Ava Barton was concerned.

Ava nodded her head sorrowfully. "I am. I wish I weren't—but I am. I agreed to do it to advance my career, because Daniel charmed the hell out of me, because I needed something to shake up my pathetic excuse for a life."

"So that explains all your doctor appointments. You weren't really sick?"

"No. I was meeting with Daniel. You were right about the secret dates. But it was a different kind of *screwing* going on."

"I'll say. You totally screwed over *Couture*," Nadine said, although her tone was kind.

"I know," Ava replied, her face twisted with regret. "And the worst part of it is, that as soon as I started, I earned a lot more respect and opportunities at *Couture* than I ever had at *Style*. Which is *so* ironic, because *Couture* is to *Style* what *Newsweek* is to the *National Enquirer*."

"So Eamon Sinds getting the big feature? The Alexander McQueen dress on Victoria Beckham? Those were because of you?"

Ava nodded solemnly. "I hate myself for doing it. It didn't take long for me to realize how wrong it all was, how I was betraying not just the friends I was making at *Couture*, but myself. I cannot believe I did this. And I tried to get out of it. At the Cutting Edge Gala, I told Daniel it was over, and for a glorious few days, I thought I was free. But it didn't work that way. He came after me. He told me that I had to honor my commitments and keep my mouth shut or he'd tell everyone that this whole spy business was my idea. We had a huge argument about it."

"Outside Bergdorf's?" Nadine asked.

"Yes. The day I went shopping for our project. I haven't reported anything since the gala, but he's still hounding me to give him the goods on our new October issue. I won't! But he's going to blow my cover and drag me down. He's going to say it's all my fault. I'll be tarred and feathered on Fashion Avenue," Ava lamented through her tears. "Daniel's a huge bigwig in this town, and I'm just Little Miss Nobody. Who's going to believe me?"

"*I will,*" Nadine said. She knew Ava was telling the truth with as much certainty as she knew that Ava really was a true friend.

"You will?" Ava asked, wiping her tears.

"I believe you, Ava. And I also believe that this Aames character is blackmailing you."

"He is?" Ava sniffled. Nadine couldn't help but notice that as miserable as Ava looked, it also seemed like the weight of her lie had been lifted.

"Damn straight he is. That Silver Fox is after you, like a real fox stalkin' chickens in a henhouse. But I got news for that operator. He's not gonna get us chickens. 'Cause we're gonna outmaneuver him."

"We are?" Ava asked.

"Oh, we most certainly are," Nadine said, a mischievous smile spreading across her face. "This little chickie's hatching us a plan."

17

Like a True New Yorker

CALLIE WOKE THURSDAY morning in a clammy sweat, her head as fuzzy as a cotton ball. She'd slept like total crap last night. August in New York City was even more brutal than humid Ohio. At least her bedroom in Columbus had air-conditioning. The dorm, on the other hand, had a wimpy fan that barely made a breeze. Every night Callie had to trick herself into frostiness by taking an icy shower before bed and lying down in front of the fan. But even that had stopped working. Last night she'd been up half the night trying to cool down by putting ice cubes on her neck, in between overthinking today's errand.

She slogged out of bed to the fridge in search of some cold water. In the dorm's tiny sitting room, she heard the low murmur of voices. That was weird. She glanced at her watch. It was seven a.m. Too early for Nadine to be up for work and too late for her to have just come home from last night's bar hop. And that other voice sounded like—Ava? What was she doing here?

Callie rounded the corner and found both girls huddled around Ava's laptop. A collection of discarded coffee cups littered the gray-carpeted floor.

"Hey, guys, what's up?" Callie asked.

Nadine snapped the laptop shut. "Oh, nothing. Work stuff."

"At seven in the morning?" Callie asked.

Ava winced guiltily. "Yeah, you know, the finishing touches on our assignment; it's been kinda crazy at work."

Finishing touches, my ass, Callie thought. She knew why they were being so secretive. It had been more than a week since her hideous meeting with Kiki and Marceline, and no one had even bothered to tell Callie she was fired; they'd just left her twisting in the wind, letting silence be her verdict. And now Ava, her new best friend, was being guarded. Obviously, there'd been some kind of directive to keep Callie out of the *Couture* loop. Well—*this* she didn't deserve! *Did she?*

"We'd probably better get going, anyway," Nadine said.

"But you don't have to be at work for three more hours. Why don't we get breakfast or something?" Callie asked. She was annoyed with their mysteriousness, but also a bit desperate for company. These last few days, roaming around alone, had been interminable. She was actually eager to get back to the bar tonight. Although she wasn't quite as eager to do what awaited her this morning.

"Sorry, Cal," Ava said, jumping up to put a consoling hand on Callie's shoulder. "We've got a crazy deadline, but I promise we'll hang out soon."

Forget *soon*. Callie planned to go back to Ohio soon. Her internship was due to end in two weeks anyhow— maybe she should give some excuse to her parents, go back a week early . . . once she earned a couple hundred more bucks at Roots, she was out of here.

Now Ava and Nadine were packing up to leave. Neither looked particularly *Couture*-worthy: no designer clothes or makeup. In fact, they looked as though they'd been up all night, their faces shining from sweat and hard work, their sundresses rumpled and disheveled.

But they grabbed their laptops, a stack of notes, some copies of *Couture* and *Style*, and were out the door before Callie had a chance to object.

She eventually went back to bed and tossed and turned for an hour more, but she was too keyed up to wait for her alarm. Besides, the dorm was like an oven. She might as well get up and get things over with.

Callie showered and carefully dressed in her favorite Callie Ryan original: a crushed-silk charcoal-gray trapeze dress with three straps across the back. On her feet, the lilac DKNY sandals that Ava had recently returned to her. Under her arms, an extra dose of Secret. She was going to need it.

Before she left, Callie hesitated over which bag to pick. She almost chickened out and grabbed a white clutch, but then she took a deep breath, summoned her courage, and plucked the Jimi Hendrix silk-screen bag out of her closet.

Riding the L train out to Brooklyn, she practiced what she was going to say. She still wasn't so sure that any of this was a wise idea. Actually, it hadn't been her idea at all but Aynsley's—which under *normal* circumstances would've been proof positive that it was the absolute worst plan in the universe. But nothing was *normal* anymore.

After Aynsley had overheard Callie's humiliating confession to Julian, she'd shocked Callie by not gloating at all. In fact, the two of them had stayed up most of Sunday night, drinking martinis and talking. That was when Aynsley suggested that Callie make peace with Quinn, the silk-screen designer, regardless of what *Couture* decided to do with her. "This is about your professional integrity," she told Callie. "You have to make it right for your own sake."

Who'd known that Aynsley was such a font of wisdom, but there you had it. And now here was Callie, standing on the corner of Bedford and North 8th, heading over to the artist's collective where she'd first met Quinn and had innocently bought his fabrics.

Williamsburg was just as fabulous as Callie remembered it, its denizens all seemingly under the age of twenty-five, every last one of them looking like they'd just walked out of a Kate Moss Topshop ad. If this hadn't been the scene of her ruin, she could have seen herself living here one day.

The loft where Quinn had his booth was just opening, with various shopkeepers raising their gates, putting out selections of handbags, dresses, jewelry, and paintings. Quinn was hanging up his collection of hats, lots of yummy whimsical turbans and twenties-style cloches. Nadine would have had a field day with his stuff, Callie mused. Callie watched him for a good five minutes, willing her legs to move her forward and her mouth to say what needed to be said.

In the end, it was Quinn who noticed her. He did a double take and then strode over to Callie on those grasshoppery skinny legs of his. "Hey there. Here for more material?" he said. His tone was joking, but Callie felt ashamed nonetheless. She hung her head and stared at her toes, which were in dire need of a pedicure.

"No. I'm here to talk to you," she muttered to the floor.

"Okay," Quinn said. "I need more coffee first. Can I get you something cold and caffeinated?"

"Umm, an iced latte?" Callie replied. She'd expected a chilly reception, but here he was offering her a chilly drink instead.

While Quinn went to the café, Callie inched over to his stall, admiring his hats. She noticed a couple of them now used his silk-screen designs. She pulled one down for a closer look. It was a screen of an Asian bamboo motif. Very funky.

"Like that one?" Quinn asked, returning with two coffees. "Reliable sources claim that silk screening is getting hot again, so I figured, why not incorporate it into my stuff, seeing as I have all this material around just gathering dust."

"Right," Callie said, fingering the metal on her own silk-screen bag. "That's what I'm here to talk to you about. The bags."

"Hey, is that one of the infamous dead celebrities? I've never actually seen one in person. Let me have a look." He grabbed the Jimi satchel from her and eyed it through his oval glasses, running his skinny fingers up and down the material. "Nice work. Very good finishes. I can see why the editors were impressed."

"You can?"

"Definitely. An eye for detail. That can't be learned."

"Um, yeah. Well, about the bags. I know it's probably a little too late, but I plan to give you all the proceeds. I mean, if I sell any of them."

Quinn shook his head. "No way!"

"But I can't do anything better than that. That's all the money I have!"

"No," Quinn said softly. "I think you misunderstand. There's no way I'm going to take all the proceeds. If anything we should just do a split. That would more than pay me back."

"Are you serious?"

Quinn shrugged. "Look. You screwed up. But as I told that editor of yours, it's not like you stole the bags. I never thought to make the silk screens into anything. And the bags are pretty cool. Marceline tells me that they've been getting lots of calls for them, so my guess is we're already sold out. And at twelve hundred bucks a pop, that's six hundred for each of us, per bag."

"The—the bags have sold out?" Callie stammered.

"Yeah," Quinn replied. "They're giving me a credit and correction in the next issue and possibly doing something on my hats, which are my first love. So we're square as far as I'm concerned. Turns out, you stealing my designs was one of the best things that's ever happened to my career. But . . . wait—you didn't know any of this?"

For some reason, Callie felt tears spring to her eyes as a jumble of emotions bucked through her. Happiness that the bags had sold. Relief that Quinn wasn't planning on suing her. Double relief because the proceeds from the sales meant she was out of debt. But also sadness, because the beginning and *end* of her career had come so quickly. There was no reason to stay in New York anymore. She might as well return to Ohio tomorrow.

"I haven't heard anything from *Couture* since the

meeting," Callie admitted mournfully. "I'm pretty sure I'm fired."

Quinn's eyed focused on her like lasers. Then his expression softened. "That's pretty harsh. But hey, if you want any more material, I'll sell it to you. I really do admire your work."

"Yeah? Well, you're probably the only one in the city," she said with a rueful laugh. "Maybe I should start a line called Career Suicide, sell it to celebrity jailbirds and other people who've screwed up their careers."

"Good to see you've got a sense of humor about it," Quinn replied. "You sound like a true New Yorker."

"I *do*?" For some reason that heartened Callie to no end.

"Definitely," Quinn said. "Hey, I think Jimi is vibrating." He handed Callie back her bag. Inside her cell phone showed that she had a text. She scrolled down to the new message. It was from Ava.

Tried 2 call. No Answer! Come to Couture NOW. URGENT Mtg. Isabel asked 4 YOU!

Callie felt a surge of hope, followed by a ripple of fear. Was it possible that Isabel was calling her in just to fire her in front of the entire staff? No—she was being paranoid. She thought back to something Aynsley had said weeks ago, when Isabel first summoned Callie to her office and Callie had been green enough to think that she was about to get fired. Back then, Aynsley had told her that bigwigs like Isabel didn't bother with firings. They got their underlings to do it. So why was she calling? Could it be that Callie was *forgiven*?

"Good news?" Quinn asked.

"I'm not sure," Callie said.

"Well, you've got this crazy grin on your face."

Callie felt her smile widen. "I don't know. But I think maybe I've got a future after all."

Quinn nodded knowingly, as if he weren't the least bit surprised by the news. "Better go grab it, then," he said.

"Experience is simply the name we give our mistakes."
—Oscar Wilde

Filed under: Fashionista > Style

The Fashionista has been getting a lot of comments on her blog recently, many of them inquiries about must-have fall items—like an ankle-length white wool Ann Demeulemeester coat. Or questions about where to pick up a cool pair of knee-high boots without going into chin-high debt—Nine West, believe it or not. My vote for sexiest jeans has been in demand, too—a tie between McQ—Alexander McQueen—and Bitten by SJP. But, rather than seeking my advice, there are some readers who'd rather chastise me for being a snob, for being too harsh in my fashion critiques, for being unwilling to accept that everyone makes mistakes.»

So let me begin with a confession: Even the Fashionista has made some terrible wardrobe calls in her day (a high-waisted wide-leg jean incident comes to mind). And I fully understand that sometimes we have to take risks to discover a new look—or we make mistakes, simply because we don't know any better.

Recently, the Fashionista came across a young designer who made a mistake and is being unfairly punished for it. She created a series of uniquely chic handbags using material silk-screened by another artist. _Couture_ magazine recently touted the bags in their Cutting Edge showcase. But, upon finding out that the young designer—a lowly _intern_ at _Couture_—didn't actually silk-screen the fabric, the magazine suspended her. I'm sure my fellow fashionistas are aware of this designer's fabulous bags, emblazoned with silk-screened images of pop culture icons. They've created quite a stir in all the chicest corners of Manhattan. Yet, it seems _Couture_ may let their gifted intern get away.

Talk about a _mistake_. Fashion's top gatekeepers are about to punish a huge talent for a youthful misstep. If _Couture_ doesn't nurture this young » designer's potential, surely someone else will. And then the Fashionista will get to enjoy watching *Couture*'s high priestesses of fashion wiping egg from their <u>Botoxed faces</u>. Won't that be a sight?

Your faithful Fashionista

18

E! True Fashion Story

THURSDAY MORNING THE *Couture* offices were a mad-house. The entire staff was on high alert, as if a current of electricity was rocketing through the halls, shocking staffers. Ava herself felt pretty damn tingly. Then again, maybe that was the sleep deprivation talking. She and Nadine had been up most of the last three nights, cobbling together their secret attack, the one that, according to Nadine, would simultaneously redeem Ava's career and launch Nadine's. It was a long shot, but Nadine seemed so certain her idea would work that Ava was caught up in her optimism. On occasion, she'd even had fun, nearly forgetting that the reason they were doing this was to undo Ava's betrayal.

"Oh, will you just quit with that whole penance thing already?" Nadine had moaned when Ava had fretted about her misdeeds. "Enough is enough. You screwed up. Now you're making good. It's the frigging American way. Haven't you ever watched *E! True Hollywood Story*? Think of this as *E! True Fashion Story*."

Ava wasn't so sure of that. She felt more like *Dead Girl Walking*, but she allowed herself to believe Nadine. They'd finished their project this morning, emailing it in at the crack of dawn. And now something was about to happen.

Isabel had called a staffwide meeting for eleven thirty, explicitly requesting that all four of the interns be present. Ava had been frantically calling Callie with no reply, but finally, at ten to eleven, she got a text, alerting her that Callie was on her way.

"So, you ready to face your maker?" Nadine asked, sidling next to Ava, who was rearranging the files on her desk for the forty-fifth time that morning. Ava checked out Nadine's ensemble—a leopard-print bustier, paired with a purple tulle tutu and a platinum blond wig—a wild choice, even by Nadine's standards. It was as though, having been dissed by the Fashionista, Nadine had decided to be even more outré. Ava admired how the girl used fashion to give a big giant middle finger to her critics. Ava, for her part, was trying to preemptively impress her critics. She'd spent a ridiculous amount of cash on a black-and-white scoopneck Tory Burch sundress. It was a dumb move—blowing savings on a dress when you were soon to be out of a job—but when Ava tried on the frock, she'd felt magically confident. In fact, sitting in the dressing room, she'd been reminded of the Cutting Edge Gala, when she'd worn that borrowed Elie Saab number and felt invincible. Ava knew that the right dress could positively transform her.

"As ready as I'll ever be," Ava replied, giving Nadine a warm smile. They were in this together now, and they both had a lot on the line.

Aynsley swept in, looking ravishing in a turquoise-and-orange cap-sleeve minidress from Custo Barcelona, paired with a funky woven turquoise straw bag she'd mentioned having picked up at a flea market.

"What is going on?" she asked breathlessly. "I just saw Kiki and I swear the woman looked like one of those zombies from *28 Weeks Later*."

"No idea. No idea whatsoever," Nadine replied with such forcefulness that Aynsley's look went from mildly curious to suddenly suspicious. She stared at Nadine and then shook her head in dismay.

"Van Buren, you are the worst liar. It's one of the things I love most about you," she added. Ava watched Nadine's mouth drop and wondered if she was going to spill the beans, but then she realized it hardly mattered. By doing what they'd done, she and Nadine had already spilled the beans. To all of New York City. To the entire fashion world.

Ava glanced at her computer's clock. Five minutes till the meeting. She wished Callie would get here already. Isabel's request to include Callie was one piece of the puzzle that Ava didn't get. Why demand *her* presence? If it meant she was back on staff, Ava was glad—but the timing was so odd. In Ava's mind, Callie's transgression still paled in light of her own lies.

Ava was just getting ready to gather her things and make her way to the conference room when a red-faced Callie burst through the door, breathing hard, as though she'd run all the way from Brooklyn.

"Oh. Good," she panted. "I thought. I was. Too late."

"You got in just under the wire," Aynsley said. "And you're sweating like a Williams sister. Better take this." She handed Callie her Chanel compact and a bottle of Fiji water.

Callie grabbed the half-full bottle and downed it before dabbing her face with powder. Ava glanced at

Callie and then back at Aynsley. So they were sharing water and makeup now? The world had truly gone mad.

"Into the conference room, you four. Now!" Kiki had suddenly materialized in the intern office, her face looking a little yellow in the reflection of her brightly colored Balenciaga dress.

"Kiki, any idea what's going on?" Aynsley asked.

"If I knew, do you think I'd be wasting my time ushering you girls into the meeting? It's all a huge mystery to me. I mean, I'm supposed to be the number three around here. Or four if you put Dieter ahead of me on the masthead, which *I* don't because our jobs are on entirely different planes—but I haven't a damn clue. Why? What do *you* know?"

Aynsley shrugged. "Me? Not a thing. I'm just an intern," she said with a modesty that was so convincing, Ava almost bought it. Ava was grateful that Kiki didn't think to ask the rest of them what was up. She just corralled them through the conference room doors and proceeded to prepare for Isabel's arrival. She admonished the staff to put away soda cans, and yelled at an assistant to hurry up with Isabel's drink. Then Dieter filed into the room looking as though he'd just bitten into a lemon, followed by Isabel's assistant with a glass of Chardonnay. A hush descended over the staff as Isabel swanned in, looking stunning in a periwinkle-blue Carolina Herrera Fils Coup dress and silvery lizard-skin Manolos.

"*Sooo,*" Isabel crooned, sitting down in her seat, an amused smile playing at the corner of her lips. "This is August. It is supposed to be a quiet time in publishing, *non*? In Paris, the magazines just shut down so everyone can relax at their chateaux. And I had hoped for a peaceful month spent in Europe or the Hamptons. But no," Isabel said, clucking her tongue. "We have more drama this month than Paris Hilton has in a year. *Mon dieu*, I like intrigue, but this is too much, even for me."

"Isabel. Can you please tell us what you're talking about?" Kiki interrupted. Isabel raised an eyebrow at her, prompting Kiki to quickly shut her mouth and slump back as though she'd been slapped.

"Perhaps our spy should do the honors," Isabel said, staring at Ava. Her violet eyes were so piercing, Ava wondered if her skin might start to burn. The entire staff then turned to her, a look of bafflement on the collective faces of *Couture*.

Isabel clapped her hands together and every eye returned to her. "No. I think I will tell the story. Or better yet. Let the magazine."

Isabel reached into her Hermès bag and pulled out a

mockup cover, not of *Couture* but of *New York* magazine. On the cover was a huge photograph of Ava, one from the "Ava on the Edge" series that Nadine had shot a few weeks ago. The cover headline read: A SPY IN THE HOUSE OF FASHION and under that: *Confessions of an intern who attempted to bring down* Couture. By Ava Barton.

The entire staff gasped, then erupted into shouts. Isabel attempted to quiet everyone down, clinking her pen against her wineglass and, when that didn't work, she put two perfectly manicured fingers into her mouth and whistled like she was calling a cab.

"*Taisez-vous! Calmez!* Be quiet!" she demanded. "Yes. Ava Barton is our mole. And yes, she had us all fooled."

Ava couldn't bear to look at Isabel or the staff. Instead, she focused her attention on her fellow interns. Nadine was blushing, hands clasped together tightly. Aynsley looked equal parts shocked and pleased about being so shocked. And poor Callie looked as though she were about to faint. She was mouthing something to herself, over and over, so Ava leaned in to hear what her friend was saying. "Wow. Wow. Wow," Callie repeated.

"Why is she still here?" Dieter demanded. "Why is she not fired? Or in jail?"

Ava winced, but Isabel was unruffled. "Well, Dieter, let me explain," Isabel said, speaking slowly as if talking to a stupid child. "For one, Ava has seen the error of her ways and has not fed any *Couture* secrets to *Style* for a few weeks now. Second of all, next week, when this article is out, news of *Style*'s treachery—and our incredible magazine's resilience—will be there for all the world to see. Needless to say, Ava's mea culpa is very kind to *Couture*. We come off smelling like gardenias."

"*Still,*" Kiki said. "Don't you think she should be punished?"

Now Isabel was looking straight at Ava, those eyes of hers boring right into Ava's soul. "I think that once you've read this article, you will understand that Ava has punished herself enough already. But, truly, I keep her with us for selfish reasons. Her writing is fantastic. Didion-esque. If I fire her, the competition will hire her, and we all lose. Sometimes in business, you have to be Machiavellian, *non?* Besides, Ava has done us a little favor. At my request, she's told Daniel Aames that we've put Kate Hudson in the most hideous Versace gown on our next cover. In response, *Style* is apparently putting Reese Witherspoon in that gown for their next issue. Poor them. By the time Ava's article comes out, it will be too late to change. *Poor Reese!*" Isabel's laughter echoed.

The room went berserk again, so Isabel clapped her hands and shouted, "*Attention!* I know there is much to discuss, but I have some other news yet. As I said, this has been quite a wild month. And this has been quite a wild batch of interns this summer, *non?*" Isabel shook her head but was also smiling. "Trouble like this also means talent. First we have Ava and her article. And then her cohort, Nadine Van Buren, whose photo of Ava is running as *New York*'s cover. Brava, Nadine! And finally we have Miss Callie Ryan."

All eyes turned to Callie, whose face had gone an almost greenish shade of white.

"I don't like that you lied about your bags," Isabel said, speaking directly to Callie now. "I would not have cared that the silk screens came from someone else. *Pff.* I don't expect designers to be textile makers. But I do expect honesty. By lying, *you*, like your friend Ava, could've harmed this magazine—which I've spent more than a decade building up."

"I know," Callie said tearfully. "I'm sorry."

Isabel waved her hands in front of her face. "Too late, too late, *ma petite cherie. But*—where before I would look foolish if I didn't fire you, *now*, I look foolish if I do!"

Ava looked at Callie, who looked so baffled, Ava thought for sure the girl would burst into tears.

"Wh-what are you *talking* about?" Callie stammered.

"Have you not read the Fashionista blog this morning?" Isabel asked, looking amazed that Callie could have missed it.

"Um, no. Not yet," Callie replied.

Isabel shook her head. "All of you should be reading this every morning," she instructed. "Right after *Women's Wear Daily*. Callie, today, you, *chère*, were the Fashionista's rant *du jour*."

"I *was*?" Callie asked, her face so pale that even her freckles seemed to disappear.

"*Oui*. Apparently, she is a big fan of your work. Her column today gushes about your many designs. It says that if *Couture* is to remain the first name in fashion innovation, we cannot ignore the talent that is right under our noses. Never mind that we featured your bags—the Fashionista says that if *Couture* doesn't hire you back, we will be, and I quote, 'wiping egg from our Botoxed faces.' So, Callie Ryan, if I don't keep you, I look like an idiot. And the fashion world suffers. So you are back on staff. Your bags are a hit. And you better make nice with that silk-screen artist, because I want more."

"I don't understand!" Callie cried. "How could this happen?"

Isabel smiled a wicked grin, and for a second Ava wondered if Isabel herself was the mystery blogger. "You may not know the Fashionista, Callie, but she clearly knows you." And with that, the meeting was adjourned.

19

Inner Bitch

WHEN, AT THE BEGINNING of the summer, Cecilia Roth-well had informed her daughter, Aynsley, that she'd called in favors to get her an internship at *Couture*, Aynsley had been miserable. *Working? Eight hours a day? Five days a week?* Could anything be more boring? Cecilia might as well have told her she'd be laboring as a fry cook at McDonald's all summer.

And yet, while Aynsley still hadn't quite got the hang of having to be at work by, *um*, ten-ish, she had to admit that her summer had been anything but dull. In fact, the drama of the last few weeks had been more tit-illating than all the who-slept-with-whom-intrigue provided by the socialite set. Aynsley filed out of Isabel's double-bombshell meeting smiling to herself, feeling as satisfied as she always did after a successful shopping stint at Barneys.

She watched the staff engaging in a gossip-fest, about Callie and the Fashionista, and Ava the mole. It was quite amusing. But after five minutes, she'd had enough. She slipped into the intern office, where she promptly kicked off her Yves St. Laurent sandals and put her feet up on her desk, savoring the silence.

But it didn't last long. "Tell me, Sly. How surprised were you?" Nadine boomed as she barreled into the room.

"Surprised about what?" Aynsley asked coyly.

"Ava as the mole. Me scoring the cover of *New York* magazine! Can you friggin' believe it?"

"Quite a coup. Congratulations," Aynsley replied sincerely. Nadine was a great photographer, and now that *New York* had confirmed it by running her shot, Aynsley knew that the girl would have many more opportunities. Which also meant an end to the tiresome pity party she'd been throwing for herself for the better half of the summer.

"Thanks. Couldn't have done it without Sam. He hooked us up with an editor at *New York*. They jumped on the idea, but we had to slam the thing together. I'm sorry I was so mysterious about the whole thing."

"No problem," Aynsley replied. "Every girl has her secrets."

"Tell me about it," Nadine said, plunking herself down next to Aynsley and kicking off her own fuzzy purple Victoria's Secret mules. "Ava as the spy? Didn't see that coming."

Neither had Aynsley. She had spent so much of her energy uncovering Callie's fakery this summer that she hadn't really bothered much with the whole espionage saga.

As if on cue, Ava entered the office, her face bashful with a do-you-forgive-me humble-pie smile. Behind her was Callie, shell-shocked and speechless.

"You guys, I just want to tell you how sorry I am. About everything," Ava began.

"Sorry. Sorry. Sorry. You are getting to be such a broken record," Nadine bellowed. "Why don't you just tattoo a giant I SCREWED UP on your forehead and stop torturing us with your contrition?"

Aynsley couldn't help but laugh. Nadine was *so* not the sentimental one.

Ava looked anxiously at Aynsley. "You're not mad, are you?"

"What do I care?" she replied. "Besides, I've met Daniel Aames before. I might have a hard time saying no to him, too. Plenty of my mom's friends have."

"You *mean* . . . ?" Ava asked.

Aynsley nodded knowingly. "Daniel's a total player. He's slept with and screwed over half the designers and editors in New York," Aynsley said. "If he weren't practically the only straight man in the fashion industry, I'm sure he'd have been run out of town years ago. So, Daniel's finally in for a taste of his own medicine. Couldn't have happened to a nicer fellow."

A smile stretched across Ava's face, though when she turned to face the still-catatonic Callie, it faded into a pained grimace. "You all right, Callie? You're not mad at me, are you?" she asked.

Callie turned to stare at Ava, her eyes wild. "I need you to tell me the truth," she croaked.

"Anything. *I swear*. My lying days are behind me."

Callie stared at Ava with squinted eyes, as if trying to see through her. "Are you the Fashionista?"

Aynsley felt a prickle run up her spine as she watched Ava's expression go from shock to amusement. Ava whooped with laughter, until she clearly saw that Callie was dead serious.

"I wish I were," Ava said. "But no. I'm not."

"You *swear*?" Callie prodded.

"I swear on *Couture*. I could barely handle *one* secret identity," Ava said with a rueful smile. "Besides, I don't know enough insidery stuff about fashion to write that blog. I mean, I'm learning so much at *Couture*. But no—I'm *not* the Fashionista."

"If you didn't write that stuff about me, who did?" Callie asked. As soon as she asked the question, the answer seemed to land on her head like a lightning bolt. She turned slowly and looked directly into Aynsley's dark, smoky eyes. Aynsley held her gaze, silently confirming Callie's suspicions and waiting to see how the girl would play her cards. But like Aynsley, Callie was a good bluffer; she didn't give a thing away.

"Naming the Fashionista will be the next mystery I solve!" Nadine bragged. "But first, Ava and I have to go to *New York* magazine to review a bunch of stuff with the fact-checker and sign our contracts."

"Have a good time," Aynsley trilled lightly, her eyes never leaving Callie's face. "I'm having a little soiree at the house tomorrow night, so cancel whatever plans you have and plan on being at the Rothwell pad at nine."

"We'll be there," Nadine and Ava chorused as they air-kissed their good-byes.

• • • • • • • • • • • •

Alone in the intern office, Aynsley and Callie engaged in a stare-off, until Callie finally broke the silence. *"Why?"* she asked.

Aynsley shrugged. "For a laugh. My mother forced this internship on me, and the blog was a great distraction from a job I didn't really want. I never meant for it to get so popular—but fashion is an incestuous little world, and sometimes the right people notice even when you're not looking for attention."

Callie's hazel eyes were ablaze as she continued to stare Aynsley down. "No. *That's* not my question. Why did you write that about *me*?" she asked in a quiet voice.

"Yeah, *that*. It's simple, really," Aynsley began. "I think you're a good designer with the potential, *maybe*, to be great. Just watching how your style evolved this summer proved that to me."

"I'm *so* confused," Callie moaned, though she couldn't help but look pleased. "Are you, like, my frenemy or something?"

"I suppose that's up to you to decide," Aynsley shot back.

"Well, you've saved my ass—twice! I took your advice and went to see Quinn. And he's forgiven me."

"Well," Aynsley replied with a smirk, "it's too bad I couldn't save you from my brother."

Callie's nose shriveled in distaste. "*Ugh*. Don't even mention him. Besides, I probably wouldn't have listened even if you'd *tried* to warn me about Julian."

Aynsley smiled. It seemed Callie had gone from a faker to a straight shooter overnight. "I know," she replied.

"I still don't get it, though," Callie countered. "You were so horrible to me all summer. How do I know I can trust the *nice* Aynsley?"

Aynsley drummed her nails on her desk. "Oh, don't you worry. There is no nice Aynsley. There's just honest Aynsley. When you started at *Couture*, you were trying way too hard, so it irritated the hell out of me."

"But, you don't know what it's like," Callie replied a tad hysterically, "to come to New York from Hicksville and try to fit in. You've never had to do that."

Aynsley had never had to prove herself to anyone; even she had to admit that it was one of the great luxuries of being who she was. But it wasn't *just* about being a Rothwell. She had plenty of rich friends who exhausted themselves trying to prove how smart, desirable, and hip they were. Aynsley, on the other hand, had always had utter faith in herself and her opinions—especially when it came to style.

"Even when you bugged the hell out of me, I still admired some of your designs," Aynsley admitted. "And then the night you and Jules had your, *ahem*, little thing, you left your portfolio—and your La Perlas—and I got a glimpse of some of your new ideas. I have to say, they knocked my Jimmy Choos off."

"So *that's* where my portfolio went."

"I have it at home. Safe and sound. But the panties, I threw *them* out," Aynsley said with a laugh. "Once I saw how much potential you have, and after we had our little chat the other night, well, I just thought maybe Isabel was being too hard on you. So . . . I did something about it."

"Aynsley Rothwell. Socialite. Crusader. Bastion of honesty?"

"Don't sound so surprised," Aynsley scolded. "It's not like a person can't have money *and* a moral compass."

"I guess you're right," Callie agreed. Then she stopped, her hazel eyes pinched and focused. "Does Isabel know that you're the Fashionista?"

"*Nobody* knows that. And I'd prefer to keep it that way. I'll take your complete silence as a token of your gratitude," Aynsley said sternly. "I did, after all, get you your internship back."

"*I* won't tell," Callie replied, her eyes dancing with the challenge. "But *you* should."

"And why ever would I do that?" Aynsley mused.

"Well . . . then you'd get to enjoy the look on Nadine's face when she finds out you're behind the Lil' Kim diss," Callie offered.

"Please, I say much worse to her face all the time. She just doesn't listen. I wrote that blog entry for her own good, though judging by today's outfit, she didn't get the message. See, this is exactly why I don't want my name to come out. If I have to start worrying about offending people, it'll muzzle my inner bitch."

"God forbid," Callie joked. Then she looked up at Aynsley to make sure it was still okay to jibe her. Aynsley allowed a small smile.

"At least tell Isabel," Callie suggested. "You don't have to go completely public, but she *clearly* respects the blog and she'd be shocked to know that you wrote it."

"I don't think so," Aynsley replied. "I prefer my anonymity."

"They're gonna find out eventually," Callie replied.

"You mean, like they discovered Ava?" Aynsley retorted. "The only reason they found Ava out was because she confessed to being a spy—in *New York* magazine, no less."

"But it's better to confess than get caught," Callie shot back. "Trust me, I know. But I'll drop it," she conceded, obviously leery of pushing Aynsley too far.

"Gee, thanks," Aynsley replied, with equal parts sarcasm and gratitude. "Although you *did* make some good points," she added flatly. She hadn't considered telling *just* Isabel before.

Callie seemed to relax in the face of Aynsley's small compliment. "Well, don't you worry. I know everyone thinks I have a big mouth, but I can keep a secret like nobody's business. I won't tell," she promised. "I mean, I know enough not to mess with your inner bitch."

A sly grin crossed Aynsley's lips in response to Callie's obvious desire not to tangle with her. "My inner bitch thanks you," she replied graciously, tossing her coal-black hair over her shoulder as she turned to go.

But, strangely enough, she didn't feel like a bitch at all.

20

A Sort of Sorcery

IT WAS ONLY THE MIDDLE of August, but already Nadine could sense the coming fall. It wasn't just that all the *Couture* editors had traded in their flowy trapeze dresses and Miu Miu sandals for this season's crop of sporty parka dresses and Dior leather boots. Nor was it that, in the span of a day, the oppressive heat had lifted, leaving clear skies and a coolish breeze in its wake. It was more about that same feeling Nadine used to have on the final days of summer camp—she felt like something was ending.

Aynsley hadn't specifically called this evening's soiree a farewell party, and there were still a few weeks left until the interns went their separate ways, but this night, too, had a kind of somberness. Normally, this kind of thing would send Nadine straight for the bar, ready to down a few shots to beat back her melancholy and bring on the party. But tonight she was sort of savoring the feeling. It was as if, in the last few weeks, the four interns had had their clothing stripped right off them. Funny thing was, now that they'd seen one another naked—flaws and all—they suddenly looked a whole lot better to one another.

Nadine stood in the parlor of the Rothwell family's grand brownstone, watching as Aynsley's well-dressed socialite pals swarmed up and down the stairs. As they flitted by, she picked up scraps of their conversations about who was sleeping with whom and which of their famous friends had hired stylists to feng shui-ify their Ivy League dorm rooms. Nadine chuckled and shook her head. Sure, she was the girl in the red vinyl miniskirt, sheer tube top, and Cleopatra wig, but as far as Nadine was concerned, she was nowhere near as freakadelic as the other company Sly kept. Suddenly, she felt two arms wrap around her neck and for a second her heart leaped. She'd asked Aynsley to invite Sam tonight. But she swiveled around to find Ava—not a bad consolation prize—looking adorable in a pair of skinny JBrand jeans and a sleeveless argyle sweater, her hair in two long braids. Tonight, Ava's smile was the best part of her outfit. After seeing Ava brooding and worried for so long, it was nice to see the girl's dimples back in full force.

"You win a puppy or something?" Nadine joked.

"Just enjoying the calm before the storm," Ava replied.

Nadine laughed. "Yeah, the shit is gonna hit the fan in the biggest of ways. Better get yourself a good umbrella."

"At least this time around, I'll have *Couture* for cover," Ava noted. "Isabel's planning a press conference when the *New York* story hits."

"I still can't believe they offered you a job!" Nadine mused.

"Staff writer," Ava said in a hushed voice. "I can't believe I'm gonna be a staff writer at *Couture*."

"No more picking up anyone's dry cleaning." Nadine laughed.

"Or Starbucks runs," Ava crowed.

"Yeah, but you're gonna have Kiki on your ass day and night. I don't envy that."

"She's okay," Ava replied, "so long as you don't barge into a meeting all bald and ranting."

"Am I *ever* gonna live that one down?" Nadine asked. Oh well, she supposed it could go in her memoir one day. She'd be a famous photographer or journalist or both, and she'd write about rising like a phoenix from her inauspicious start. To be honest, she couldn't quite believe how low she'd sunk this summer or how high she'd bounced back. She'd shot a *New York* magazine cover. She'd shot models for fashion shoots. She even had representation, thanks to Sam, who'd recommended Nadine to his photo agency.

"If I can live down Daniel, you can live down your hair trauma," Ava said confidently. "And speaking of trauma, I'd better go find Callie. She's still looking at me like I just announced I'd had a sex change or something. I really shocked the poor girl."

"Damn, you even shocked me," Nadine replied. "And I'm a hell of a lot less innocent than Callie."

"Hey, baby! You're here." Charging up to Nadine were Hayden and Spencer, Aynsley's two indistinguishable prepster friends clad in matching Abercrombie & Fitch. She'd alternated between hooking up with one or the other of the pair all summer long. "What are you drinking? Is that mineral water?" asked a horrified Hayden.

"Hey, guys," Ava said, retreating. "I'll catch you

later," she mouthed to Nadine before backing down the stairs and toward the garden.

"Yeah, Nadine. Don't tell me you've gone twelve-step on us?" Spencer asked.

"Nah. Just chillin' a bit," Nadine replied.

"Well, stop chillin' and start heatin'. Here," Hayden said, shoving his flask in Nadine's face.

"Nah. I'm cool. I'll grab a beer in a second."

"Forget beer. I've got some of my father's finely aged single malt Scotch in here," Hayden said, shaking his monogrammed flask. "Two hundred bucks a bottle."

"No thank you," Nadine replied sternly, pushing the flask out of her face.

"What's the matter, Cleopatra?" Spencer asked with a toothy grin. "Don't you wanna party with the big boys tonight?"

Once upon a time, Nadine would've responded to a challenge like that by brazenly grabbing the flask and downing all that expensive booze in one gulp. Except the strangest thing was, she no longer felt like she needed to prove anything to anyone, except maybe herself.

Nadine pulled back her shoulders and gave the boys her best Jada-Pinkett-Smith don't-even-*think*-of-screwing-with-me face. "Just the opposite," she said. "I don't wanna party with the *little* boys ever again." And with that she flounced down the stairs, no easy feat in the purple Christian Louboutin five-inch heels she'd liberated from Sly's closet a few hours back.

The party was a swirl of beautiful people, each one dressed in an outfit that probably cost more than a month's rent back in Nadine's hometown. Everyone was sipping Flirty Sluts, the signature drink that Aynsley had concocted for the night. But Nadine didn't feel much like gossiping, or downing Flirty Sluts, or even being a flirty slut. She grabbed an Amstel from the bartender that Aynsley had hired for the night and plucked a smoked salmon canapé from the buffet before sitting down on a bench under a jasmine vine.

"Do not even tell me that you're doing the wallflower thing again," Aynsley said, balancing two martinis in one hand and two Flirty Sluts in the other.

"Nah. Just resting my feet. These shoes are killers."

"Fashion hurts," Aynsley said with a smirk. "No one ever said looking good was easy."

"You make it look easy," Nadine quipped. "With a little help from Gregory Rothwell. How much did that dress cost you?"

"This little thing?" Aynsley said, twirling in her funky, flowy, floor-length, backless white halter dress. "Not a thing. It's vintage Valentino, courtesy of Mom's closet. It's from her Studio 54 days. Believe it or not, back before she was a chintz-loving, Chanel-suited matron, she actually had a modicum of style."

"Sly, even when you wear freebies, you look like the richest girl in the room," Nadine said.

Aynsley eyed her friend with a smirk. "Making it look easy is the hardest part. Like my new Alaïas?" she asked, showing off a pair of studded gladiator sandals, the cost of which Nadine suspected more than made up for the thriftiness of the dress. She'd have to borrow those before the summer was out.

"Anyhow, I must go be a proper hostess, but I'll see you later," Aynsley said. "And I expect you to dance, drink, and be Van Buren-y."

"You got it," Nadine promised.

As Aynsley flitted back to her hostessing duties, Nadine sat back, closed her eyes, and inhaled the sweet scent of the white flowers trellised above her head. Suddenly, she felt someone watching her. Expecting Aynsley, Nadine opened her eyes to find Sam Owens, looking downright edible in skinny Dickies and a worn cashmere sweater. He was staring at her, smiling, and shaking his head.

"What'd I do?" Nadine asked.

Sam continued smiling. "What did *I* do? Forgot my

bloody camera is what. What's the point of being a photographer if you don't have your equipment ready when the perfect shot of a pretty girl is right in front of your eyes?"

A feeling of warmth flooded Nadine's chest. She smiled, sat forward, and licked her lips, admiring Sam's intelligent blue eyes, his kissable lips so red they looked like he had lipstick on. "You could always take a snap with your phone," she suggested.

"Wouldn't do you justice," Sam replied. He motioned to the bench where she was perched. "Mind if I sit down? I haven't seen much of you this past week."

"I know," Nadine replied, scooting over to make room. "Ava and I were working twenty-four/seven on that story. Thanks for offering up your connections on that, by the way."

"I'm glad it worked out. And delighted that you got the cover of *New York*. At, what—age seventeen? Not even I have that kind of record."

Nadine tilted her head closer to Sam, happy to smell his baby powder scent. "I'm not seventeen, Sam. I'm eighteen. And I'll be nineteen on October thirty-first."

"Halloween? Why am I not surprised?" Sam laughed.

"You calling me a witch?"

"*Nah*—but you do have a sort of sorcery thing going on."

"Yeah, it's more like a hex," Nadine corrected him. "Or a dumb kid playing with a magic kit." Her tone was joking, but deep down she was serious.

"Trust me, Nadine. You are many, many things, but a dumb kid is not one of them."

Nadine's heartbeat sped up. "What am I, then?" she asked.

"I think you're quite amazing, really," Sam said in a funny strangled voice.

"You do?" Nadine replied, her eyes flicking up to Sam's adorably embarrassed face.

"Amazing, but perhaps a bit thick. I mean, what does a guy have to do? Help you with a photo shoot, get Zehna to model your concept, hook you up with *New York* magazine?"

"But I thought you were just doing all that because you felt sorry for me."

"Hardly," Sam replied.

"But, I totally threw myself at you at the gala and you didn't respond."

"Well, for one, I had to worry about being professional. The entire staff was there. And for another, if memory serves, you were so drunk you would likely have thrown yourself at Dieter."

"Now, honey," Nadine replied with a laugh, "I've never been *that* drunk."

"Good to know," Sam replied. "But you did spoil the mood a little when you threw up on me."

"Don't remind me," Nadine groaned. "But what about that day in the Bronx? You came right out and said you didn't want or expect *anything* in return."

"That's right. I didn't want you to think it was all some kind of come-on. I am dead serious about your potential as a photographer, but that was just the thing. The way you talk, dress, piss people off—not to mention the photos you take—there's only so much a bloke can resist."

A thousand sassy, sexy responses flew through Nadine's mind, but none of them made it through to her mouth. She was too busy reeling from Sam's confession, not entirely trusting that he meant what she hoped he meant.

"Do I have to spell it out for you?" Sam asked. "All right, then. Nadine, I'm completely falling for you."

"You are?" Nadine had barely admitted, even to herself, how much she liked Sam. She'd crushed on him, lusted after him, admired him, and genuinely liked him. But with all the rejection she'd suffered this summer, she hadn't let herself imagine that he'd do anything but turn her down flat.

"I'm a goner," Sam replied.

"Well," Nadine began. "To quote my favorite Englishman, it's about bloody time."

Sam looked at her, his eyes amused, playful, and sincere all at the same time. Nadine leaned in, but Sam just continued to stare.

"So, are you gonna take a picture or kiss me?" she demanded.

Sam seemed only too happy to oblige. He leaned in and Nadine finally felt the irresistible softness of his lips.

Now, this, she thought, *is more than worth the wait.*

THE Fashionista

HOME   GOSSIP   FORUMS   CONTACT

"Don't compromise yourself. You're all you got."
—Janis Joplin

Filed under: Fashionista > Style

The Fashionista realizes there are circumstances in life that force us to bend to someone else's will—be it following a boss's insipid orders, obeying a parental curfew, or agreeing to go to a hockey game with a boyfriend. But there are two aspects of your life that you need never compromise: your true self and your true style. And really, one should organically grow from the other.

So, if you're a tomboy at heart (perhaps you even *enjoy* the occasional hockey game), then feel free to avoid <u>tulle skirts and lacy camisoles</u>, no matter how much the rage they are this season. And if » you're a bona fide <u>Fancy Nancy</u>, then there's no reason to worry when shoe trends turn to <u>flat-heeled '80s punk boots</u>. Just ignore them!

Now, the Fashionista is not suggesting that tomboys live in <u>tracksuits</u>, any more than I'm extolling divas who don <u>ball gowns</u> at the office. But every season yields a look to accommodate your own individual style. Casual chicas can chill out this fall in <u>tight black cords</u>, <u>crisp collared shirts</u>, and <u>well-cut leather jackets</u>. And there's a new crop of <u>retro, fur-lined, bias-cut dresses</u>, jackets, and skirts to make girly girls blissful, too.

To know your style is to know yourself—it all comes down to that. It *always* comes down to that. No matter how unreal an outfit may be, you won't wear it well, like a true Fashionista, unless the girl underneath is being real.

Until next time.

Your faithful Fashionista

21

Blinded by the Glam

AVA WAS ON HER THIRD Flirty Slut of the night. Which might possibly have explained why she'd just done what she'd done.

She'd written her first unofficial message on the brand-spanking-new BlackBerry that Kiki had given her that morning. "Welcome to *Couture*'s staff; here's your leash," Kiki had said with a sarcastic grimace as she'd handed the BlackBerry over. Ava could tell that Kiki was still livid over the spying revelation. Many staffers were. So Ava knew she'd have to prove her trustworthiness and talent a hundred times more than any other new staffer—but even if she had to work fifteen-hour days to do it, she *would* do it.

But there was someone else Ava had to make things up to. Which is why, after trying in vain to find Callie, and after downing her third fruity-but-potent cocktail, she'd suddenly grabbed her BlackBerry out of her Fendi Silver and quickly dashed off a note to Reese. The message was simple: the link to the article in *New York* magazine, which would go live Monday, and two sentences. *I'm sorry I blew you off. This article won't excuse my behavior—but it should help explain it.*

After she hit Send, she felt a huge surge of relief. It wasn't that she expected a response—she didn't know much about guys, but she had few illusions that someone as cute, smart, and talented as Reese would stay on the market for long. At least the article was a first step in clearing the air and making it up to all the people she'd wronged.

Ava slipped her BlackBerry back into her bag and did a loop around the Rothwell garden. She'd known Aynsley was rich, but she'd never, ever expected this kind of opulence. The house was about three times as big as her parents' suburban spread, had more old furniture than a year's worth of *Antiques Roadshow*s, and enough priceless paintings to start an art museum. The English-style garden was crammed with partyers, their faces illuminated by the tiki torches flickering around the perimeter of the deep yard. Ava pushed her way through the throngs to the buffet table, and Callie snuck up behind her.

"I'm gonna fill up on sushi tonight," Callie confessed. "They don't have the good stuff in Columbus."

Callie! Ava was so happy to see her friend, standing next to her, talking to her, that she had the urge to tackle her in a huge hug. But she still wasn't sure how things stood between them. She'd already explained to Callie that she hadn't meant to deceive her, but Callie's only response had been to nod and say "uh-huh" over and over. So Ava wasn't sure if she'd really gotten through to her. Still, if all Callie wanted was to play it casual and talk about sushi, Ava was content to follow her lead.

"Well, this fish doesn't come from New York, anyway," Ava said. "They fly the stuff in."

"I know that—it's more of a psychological thing," Callie admitted.

"Have I told you yet how much I love your dress?" Ava asked. Callie was wearing a chic belted deep purple tunic dissected by a row of buttons.

"Thanks," Callie said. "It's a total knockoff of a Rebecca Taylor dress I saw but couldn't afford." Callie grinned and threw her arms up into the air as if to say *I surrender*. "I may not have money but at least I know how to sew."

"That's probably *why* you know how to sew. Necessity is the mother of invention, and all," Ava replied.

"That's totally true. One of my favorite things that I made this summer is a camisole with a beaded flower that I sewed on to hide a lipstick stain—compliments of Nadine."

"See what I mean?" Ava said, feeling relieved that she and Callie seemed to be on solid ground. "Aynsley may have a great wardrobe, but I doubt she could sew on a button."

"Oh, I don't know. I'll bet she's got some tricks up her sleeve," Callie said, smiling mysteriously. "Hey, shove over," she added, playfully bumping Ava's hip. "You're blocking the California rolls."

Ava laughed and inched over. Out of the corner of her eye she caught a glimpse of Nadine in the shadows. Then she did a double take. Nadine was in a hot-and-heavy embrace with Sam. They stopped to chat and giggle, and then kissed some more. As Ava watched them, she felt truly happy for Nadine—and only slightly jealous. Would it ever be her turn to get the guy?

"Well, well, well. Nadine got her man," Callie murmured approvingly.

"Have you ever been in love?" Ava asked wistfully. It seemed like the whole world had, except for her.

Callie stared hard at her unagi roll. "I don't think so. I mean, I thought I was, but now I think it was more of a lust thing. Have you?"

Ava laughed. "Are you kidding? I've never had a boyfriend. Barely a date, even."

"So that was all true?" Callie asked, twirling a piece of her thick, tawny hair.

"Yep. At this rate I'm destined to be a forty-year-old virgin."

Callie stared hard at Ava through narrowed eyes. "I wasn't sure whether the virgin story was part of your whole act," she said. "A way to gain our trust."

Ava shook her head vehemently, whipping her braids around. "Callie, I need you to understand that everything you learned about me this summer is still true. Our friendship is still true. And I didn't fake my feelings, my thoughts, or my ambitions. I just lied about my job."

"Well, at least that makes one of us. I lied about all sorts of stuff," Callie said blithely.

"But I don't feel like you lied to me," Ava said. Sure,

Callie had fibbed about her background and omitted a few important details about the handbags, and maybe it was all relative, but these kinds of details seemed insignificant to Ava. "I feel like the real you, the one I whispered with way into the night, the one who helped me out from the beginning, is the *true* you."

"She is. One of them, anyhow. But that's nice of you to say," Callie said, her mouth stretching into the first genuine smile of the evening. "So I take it that you and Reese never went out."

"No. I took the dress for *Style*. You assumed I borrowed it for a big date and part of me was only too happy to pretend it was true."

"Too bad. He was a cutie. But I'm sure there'll be other guys. You're gonna be the hot new writer at *Couture*. They'll be swarming."

"All six of the straight men in fashion, you mean?" Ava joked.

"Make that five," Callie replied, motioning toward Nadine and Sam. "Van Buren appears to have taken one out of circulation."

Ava was glad to see that Callie had her sense of humor back. Actually, come to think of it, Callie seemed more comfortable than ever. Maybe that was the benefit of hitting rock bottom—the only place to go from there was up.

"So you and I," Ava began, "we're okay? You're not still mad at me or freaked out?"

"I was never mad at you," Callie explained. "It was just that there was so much going on, my head was ready to explode. Besides, how could I be pissed at you for lying when I did the same thing? We were both just trying to claw our way to the top."

Ava nodded. She'd never thought of herself as an ambition-obsessed diva, but when she was on the outside looking in, she had been totally blinded by the glam. Now that she was on the inside looking out, she knew it was the truth alone that had gotten her here.

"That said," Callie added with a gleam in her eyes, "I wouldn't say no to an article about me when I've got something new and fabulously original to release."

"You got it," Ava promised. "But I don't think you'll need me. You've been written up in *Couture*. And praised by the Fashionista. You're in the same league as Donna Karan now."

"Ha. Maybe one day."

"Yeah, one day," Ava replied, her gaze drifting back to Nadine, who was now curled up on Sam's lap, laughing.

"They're pretty cute, but they should get a room,"

Callie joked. She turned to look at her friend and reached out and squeezed her hand. "Don't worry, Ava. Our turn will come. But for now, maybe we should savor the things we have rather than worrying about the things we don't."

22

Beware of
Well-dressed Pond Scum

CALLIE'S MOM USED TO SAY that you could tell how good a party was by how long it took for someone to spill a drink on you. Using that logic, tonight's soiree was already a fantastic success. Callie had been in the Rothwell mansion for less than an hour before one of Aynsley's socialite pals managed to dump an entire Bloody Mary down the front of her dress.

"Oh my god. I'm so sorry!" the girl cried. "I'm a total klutz. And look at your dress. Is it ruined?"

Callie shook her head. "Nothing a little soda water and soap won't fix," she said, making her way toward the kitchen sink.

The socialite followed her, apologizing. "I hope I didn't ruin it. It would be such a shame because that is simply the most adorable dress. Marc Jacobs?"

"No, I made it," Callie admitted. "Loosely based on a Rebecca Taylor design."

The socialite fingered the fabric. "I was at Rebecca Taylor last week and I didn't see anything half as cute as this. *Are you a designer?*"

Oddly enough, this was the first time all summer long that someone had asked Callie if she was a designer. Back in Columbus, she had stood in front of her bedroom mirror and practiced introducing herself as a hotshot Midwestern designer and a force to be reckoned with. But now that the question had finally come, she wasn't sure how to reply. "I think I'm on my way to becoming one," she said. As an experiment of sorts, she was giving the whole blatant truth thing a whirl.

"I'd say you're already there. What's your name, so I can keep an eye out for your stuff? And please let me give you some money for dry cleaning."

"Not necessary," Callie insisted. "I know a million stain-removal tricks. Dry cleaners are a last resort. And my name is Callie Ryan."

The socialite twitched her aquiline nose, narrowed her blue eyes, and ran her slender fingers through her blond highlights. "That name rings a bell. Do you summer in Quogue?"

"I've never been to Quogue," Callie replied. "I'm an intern at *Couture*."

The girl continued to study her. "Oh my god! You're the one the Fashionista wrote about! Fashionista didn't say your name, but it's all over the Internet. I can't believe I'm meeting you. Oh, goodness. Where are my manners? I'm Sabrina. Sabrina Warren. I'm just beside myself. I live for that blog."

"Yeah, me too," Callie said with a grin.

"This is so exciting. It's almost like meeting the Fashionista herself, whoever she is. I've got to tell someone. Hey, Julian. Jules, get over here!" She turned to Callie. "That's Julian Rothwell. I had a fling with him one year in Gstaad, only to find out he was also romancing my best friend. He's such a cad," she said, laughing.

Julian approached, a broad grin on his face. He kissed Sabrina on both cheeks, while looking right at Callie.

"Julian, this is Callie Ryan. She was just written up by the Fashionista. I had to tell *someone*, so I've settled for you!"

Julian let the insult sail over him. "Oh was she?" Julian said, a flirtatious grin plastered on his handsome face. "I don't know what that is, but it sounds awfully important."

"Oh, look, there's Tinsley. I simply must tell her that I'm now one degree of separation from the Fashionista. So good to meet you, Callie," Sabrina said, offering her hand. And then she was off.

Callie looked up at Julian, who was still smiling at her, as if the other night had never happened. Actually, *that* was kind of strange, because Callie, too, felt like it had never happened. Her humiliating confession. Aynsley's bedroom tirade. Their summer of flirtation. Staring at Julian now, Callie felt nothing. Not a sparkle of lust. Not a hint of mortification. Julian grabbed her hand and leaned in for a kiss. But Callie dodged his face, making him air-kiss her ear.

"Babe, I've missed you," Julian began, going full throttle with his schmoozy charm. "It's been a lonely week."

"Oh, *really?*" Callie replied. "It seemed you couldn't wait to get away from me the last time we were together."

Julian shook his head. "I know this seems hard to believe, but I'm such a sensitive guy that it's really difficult for me to see people I care about in pain."

"Oh, you felt too much for me?" Callie asked sarcastically.

"Absolutely. But I've been keeping tabs on you. Aynsley told me you're back at *Couture*. And now you've been written up by The Fashionator."

"The Fashion*ista*," Callie corrected. Julian was even worse at talking fashion than he was at playing the concerned boyfriend.

"Right. And you know, I turned down a sailing trip in Greenwich this weekend to come to this party, hoping I'd run into you," he said, running his hand up Callie's bare arm.

"Oh, *did you?*" Callie nudged her arm away.

"To be honest, my big hope was that I'd see you here tonight and squire you away for the weekend. We could go sailing. Do you know how to sail?"

Callie did not. She'd never been on a boat, aside from a canoe or rowboat. Sailing was, in fact, on the list of things she'd hoped to do someday, along with living in Italy, meeting Donna Karan, and getting her designs into *Couture* magazine. A few weeks ago, Callie would've sold her left arm to go sailing with Julian. But that was then; this was now. And it wasn't *just* that Julian had been a total asshole after she'd slept with him, or that he'd been completely insensitive in the face of her big confession.

As Callie had just told Ava a few minutes ago, she

planned to start relishing what she had. And as for the things she wanted, they'd come. All in good time.

"So, Jules. Do you know what we call people like you in Ohio?" Callie drawled.

"I didn't know they had a name for people like *me* in Ohio," he joked.

Callie licked her lips seductively and jutted her shoulders back. "Oh, but they do," she cooed. And then, raising her voice into a semi-shout so that everyone in the vicinity could hear, she said, "In Ohio, we call guys like you *pond scum*. You know, after the bottom-dwelling, parasitic, slimy crap that squishes beneath your feet, grosses you out, and makes you feel like you need a shower. That's what you are, only prettied up. Ladies, beware of well-dressed pond scum!"

Several titters echoed through the kitchen. A flicker of panic infiltrated Julian's suave façade, but he quickly covered it up with a slick smile. "Come on, babe. Don't be like that. I'll make it up to you. How about we get out of here and grab some dinner at Nobu?" he said, reaching for her hand. "I know you've been dying to go there."

Callie snatched her arm away. "I don't think so," she said loudly. "Honestly, Jules, I'm out of your league." And with that she turned on her heel and pranced out of the kitchen, past a cadre of stunned and amused-looking partygoers. Among them was Sabrina Warren, who smiled and winked at Callie as she passed. Feeling the need for some fresh air, Callie marched out to the garden, where Aynsley, a smirk eating up her entire face, was waiting for her. She raised one of her thin bangled arms in the air and gave Callie a high-five.

"Do you eavesdrop on *all* my conversations?" Callie joked.

"Just the juicy ones," Aynsley replied with a laugh. "*Pond scum*. That was rich. You mind if I use it?"

"It's all yours," Callie replied.

"I heard you *bumped* into Sabrina," Aynsley said, motioning inside toward the klutzy socialite. "She's been swooning about your dress, and she's told half the girls here about you. That girl's mouth and her trust fund have made more careers than *Couture*."

"Well, I guess the gods were smiling on me when they sent her drink flying onto my dress," Callie replied. "And speaking of gods and *Couture*, would you *please* reconsider talking to Isabel?"

Aynsley smiled mysteriously and then pressed a finger to her pursed lips. She beckoned for Callie to follow her into a small room off the kitchen that was full of cleaning supplies, then she shut the door, muffling the din of the partyers outside.

"Can't be too careful," she said. "Lots of loose lips around here."

"Mine are sealed," Callie promised. "So I'm guessing from the look on your face, you've talked to Isabel? What did she say?"

"It was the oddest thing, but Isabel said she suspected I was the Fashionista all along." Aynsley shrugged her petite shoulders. "I don't know if that's true or if she just likes to sound in the know. But old Isabel just arched her eyebrows at me, like she'd been waiting for me to make the announcement."

"And that was that?"

"That was that," Aynsley confirmed.

"*Oh*," Callie said. She didn't know why, but she'd somehow hoped that telling Isabel would do something more for Aynsley, not that Aynsley Rothwell needed anyone's help.

"Look at you," Aynsley said. "You're so disappointed. I'm touched. Okay, I'm going to tell you the rest of it, but you cannot repeat it to a soul. You, me, and Isabel will be the only ones who know."

Callie was flattered to be included in such an exclusive trio. She swore herself to secrecy.

"Isabel wants to add my blog to *Couture*'s website—maintaining my anonymity. She says it will *only* work if the Fashionista's identity remains a mystery. And, on top of that, she's going to launch a new shopping column called 'Our Girl on the Street' and she's hired me, *as myself*, to travel around the country and report on great shopping in different cities." Aynsley paused in wonderment, as if unable to comprehend her own good fortune. "She's giving me a contract and everything. I *cannot* believe someone is going to pay me to shop."

Callie shook her head and laughed. Leave it to Aynsley Rothwell to score such a charmed job. A few days ago, this news would've made Callie seethe with jealousy. But now, after all that had happened, and after Aynsley saving her butt, she tried her best to be happy for her. "That is pretty incredible," Callie mused. "Congratulations."

"Thanks. I start right after Labor Day. And I'm finally going to get my own apartment and have my own life. Gregory and Cecilia will be none too pleased that I'm skipping college. But so what? Anna Wintour didn't go to college——"

Suddenly, the door was flung open and a drunken couple staggered in, giggling. "We're just looking for a little privacy," the guy slurred. "The rooms upstairs are locked."

Aynsley rolled her eyes and grabbed Callie's arm,

pulling her out of the little room. "That's because I locked all the bedrooms," she whispered into Callie's ear. "Cecilia's still furious about the Léron sheets that were ruined during Julian's last party. I'm so much more responsible than him."

"Trust me, I'm aware of who the superior sibling is," Callie said knowingly.

"Well, I'm going to do some damage control. But grab Ava and Nadine—if you can detach her from Sam—and meet me on the top floor in fifteen. There's a balcony off Gregory and Cecilia's bedroom with amazing views of the city."

"Sure," Callie said with a laugh. "It sounds like the perfect spot for four girls on their way up."

23
Truth and Fashion

AYNSLEY SURVEYED THE PARTY. Guests were dancing, chatting, hooking up—all as it should be. Her job was done. *Let Jules play host for a while.* She slipped down into the basement wine cellar and grabbed a bottle of 1995 Krug Clos du Mesnil. At $750 a bottle, her father wouldn't be too pleased to learn that Aynsley had taken one of his prized bubblies, but Aynsley meant to celebrate tonight. And if she had to pay him back, she'd soon be able to. With her *own* money.

She nuzzled the champagne into a bucket of ice, grabbed four crystal flutes, and climbed to the second floor. She was careful to make sure that only the doors to Jules's bedroom and the bathrooms were left open.

On the third floor, she used her master key to open her bedroom door. When she was younger it seemed so unfair that Gregory and Cecilia had the power to lock or unlock any door in the house. It was just another way that they ruled her life. But by the time she'd started throwing parties, she realized that locks had benefits. And, soon enough, she'd be the only one ruling her life.

She wandered into her closet, trading her Alaïa sandals for a pair of super-comfy ballet flats. Then she sat on her Japanese-style platform bed. Aynsley loved her room. So stark and serene. Wherever she moved to next—a loft in Soho, perhaps?—she planned to decorate the entire place modern and minimalist, completely the opposite of her mother's gilt palace. Just pondering picking out her own furniture, paint colors, and wall art sent a ripple of excitement through her so intense that it actually gave her the chills.

Locking her room up tight, Aynsley padded over to her parents' suite and turned on the light. She opened the French doors onto the balcony, laid the champagne on a small wrought-iron bistro table, and lit a dozen votive candles.

"Oh, honey, aren't you romantic?" Nadine said,

standing in the doorway with the goofiest grin in the world on her face.

"I think you've had enough romance for tonight," Aynsley joked. "Shall I unlock a guest room for you and Sam?"

"Nah. That can wait till later. And, besides, I told him tonight's for chilling with my girls, so he's taking me out *tomorrow* night."

"Whatever will you wear? It'll be hard to top that ensemble," Aynsley said with the barest hint of disdain. By now, Nadine was used to Aynsley dissing her style, and by now Aynsley was used to Nadine ignoring her.

"I might have to borrow those shoes you had on earlier," Nadine suggested. "And, by the way, Sam likes my style." She walked to the balcony's edge and called out into the city, *"So, Fashionista, wherever you are, you can kiss my finely shaped ass!"*

Aynsley smiled, savoring her secret. "I see. And I see Sam left you with a little souvenir of your first hookup," Aynsley said, pointing at a little purple welt on Nadine's neck.

"That's nothing compared to what I did to him," Nadine bragged.

"I'm glad things are working out for you," Aynsley said warmly.

"And now we can work on getting *you* some action," Nadine suggested. "I'm beginning to suspect you're some kind of nun. And *by the way,* what is the deal with you and Callie? I've never seen you so *buddy-buddy*."

Aynsley shrugged. She loved Van Buren, but somehow what had transpired between her and her former nemesis seemed private. "The drama was getting tiresome" was all she said.

"Wow! Does your mother like pink or what?" Callie announced as she and Ava trotted onto the balcony. "That bedroom set! Pink satin bedspread, pink satin headboard, pink satin bed skirt?"

Aynsley nodded. "Mother was going for the whole Bette Davis 1940s motif, but I think the room looks like the inside of a Pepto-Bismol bottle."

"Your father must be a tolerant man," Ava said with a laugh. "This view is incredible!"

The girls all turned to look out on Manhattan. From the balcony, a break in the buildings on Fifth Avenue opened onto a view that stretched west across Central Park to the jutting ornate towers of the San Remo and south to the jumble of skyscrapers in midtown. Off in the distance was the silver spike of the Conrad Media building, the place where their summer together began.

"I love it up here," Aynsley said. "Some people say New York is ugly, but I've been to Paris, Rome, Tokyo, and none of them has one ounce of Manhattan's beauty."

"Biggest small town in the world," Nadine added.

"It seems so peaceful from up here," Ava said. "You'd never guess there were so many people and so much intrigue lurking out there."

"At the beginning of the summer when I'd just flown in, I was taking a cab into the city from the airport," Callie chimed in. "And just before you go into the Midtown Tunnel, there's this big panoramic view of Manhattan. I remember thinking that as soon as I came out on the other side of that tunnel, I was finally going to be a part of it all—and my life would never be the same again."

Aynsley had always lived in New York. She'd never been awestruck by the city. But oddly enough, she was feeling the same tingle, the same sense of possibility that Callie described. Though her future was still nebulous, it excited her in a way that nothing—save for a new pair of Christian Louboutins or a Stella McCartney dress—had in years.

"Now that you've sold all your handbags, maybe you can afford to take a limo to the airport when you go home," Nadine said with a sly smile.

Callie slapped her hand to her forehead. "Don't even talk to me about going home. I can't imagine being back in Ohio. I mean, even with all the awful things that happened this summer." Callie paused and shot Aynsley a quick look. "I don't want to be anywhere else. I wish I could just stay here, move to Williamsburg. Start designing."

"Maybe you can. Stranger things have happened," Aynsley said, returning Callie's private glance.

"Yeah, like me and Sam getting together. Isn't he just the perfect man?" Nadine asked.

"Yes, Nadine, *he's perfect*," the girls intoned together.

"Besides, Callie," Ava said, "it's not like you're going home just yet. And you can come visit whenever you want. You can stay with me. I have a cute studio in Gramercy Park."

"You do?" all the girls asked in unison.

Ava nodded her head and laughed. "I forgot how much you don't know. I've been subletting my studio for the summer so I could move into the dorm with the two of you. Daniel thought it would make me seem more credible. And the dorm's a lot cheaper than my apartment—not to mention a little bigger."

Aynsley thought to mention that Callie would be

welcome at her own, more spacious new apartment, wherever that ended up being. But she wasn't quite ready to be that chummy yet. And besides, an invitation would require an explanation.

"Sly, you aging that champagne for another few years or are we gonna drink it?" Nadine asked.

"Patience, Van Buren. I was just chilling it." Aynsley reached over and felt the neck of the bottle. It was cold. She expertly popped the cork, filling up the four flutes and handing them to Nadine, Callie, and Ava. "What shall we toast to?" she asked.

"To New York!" Callie shouted.

They clinked glasses and drank.

"To *Couture*," Ava added, and they clinked again.

"Ohh, my turn," Nadine said. "To men!"

"I don't know about that one," Callie replied. "I'm not feeling quite so warm and fuzzy about the opposite sex right now."

"I said 'men,' not 'boys,'" Nadine responded. "Julian's a kid—no offense, Sly."

"Daniel was a man," Ava pointed out. "And he wasn't any good, either."

"He was a snake," Nadine insisted. "And it's *my* toast. So, to men!"

"To men!" the girls relented, laughing.

"And to success," Nadine added. "Don't want you all to think that I only care about guys."

"To success," they mimicked, clinking and drinking again.

Callie looked at Aynsley. "What about you? What are you toasting to?"

Aynsley didn't have to think twice. She held up her champagne, the golden liquid glowing in the candlelight. "To truth," she declared.

"To truth," the girls repeated. Callie and Ava caught each other's eye in a meaningful exchange.

"And to fashion," Aynsley added.

"To truth and fashion!"

They clinked glasses one final time and drank their champagne while the lights of New York City glittered all around them.

HOME   GOSSIP   FORUMS   CONTACT

"I cannot and will not cut my conscience to fit this year's fashions."—Lillian Hellman

Filed under: Fashionista > Style

Sure, the Fashionista lives to see the delectable new clothes, shoes, and accessories that designers parade down the runway each season. But like the brilliant American playwright Lillian Hellman, quoted above, I'd never put my conscience aside to shill for a trend I didn't fully believe in. There is a vast difference between accepting blisters on your feet so you can wear the latest pair of Gucci stiletto boots, and sacrificing your integrity in the name of fashion— or in the name of *anything* for that matter.

For those of you who haven't seen it in Gawker or read it on Page Six, there are some changes » afoot for the Fashionista. My blog will soon relocate to _Couture_ magazine's website.

Couture has long been an essential source for Fashionistas of all kinds, but occasionally even fashion luminaries need a little shaking up. And that's where the Fashionista comes in.

To my detractors, crying "sellout," I say this: Just because _Couture_ is hosting my blog it does not mean that the glossy now owns the Fashionista. In fact, only one person at the magazine even knows who I am, and my confidante's lips are hermetically sealed.

So, the Fashionista will continue to cast an unapologetic eye on all that is glorious and gauche in this crazy fashion world, even if it means occasionally biting the manicured hand that feeds me. And here's my first nip: _Couture_'s fall feature on aviator glam is positively tired and ridiculous. What were they smoking up there?

Now, hear this: The Fashionista vows to keep her eyes peeled, her mind open, and to never, ever muzzle her inner bitch.

More to come . . .

Your faithful Fashionista

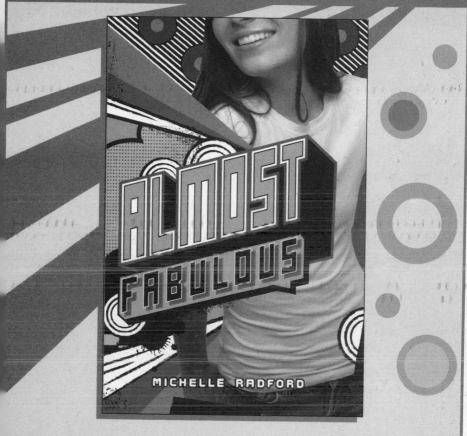

Welcome to Wellington: Just because you're rich, brilliant, and perfect in every way doesn't mean you can survive boarding school.

Check out the first three novels in the Upper Class series!

The Upper Class

No one ever thinks they'll crash and burn in their first semester—but someone always does.

Laine is a born Wellington girl: rich, sophisticated, blond. Nikki is everything a Wellington girl shouldn't be: outlandish, sexy, from a new money family. Laine and Nikki couldn't have less in common. But to survive first semester, they may have to stick together—or risk being the first girl to go down in flames.

Miss Educated

Just because you survived first semester doesn't mean you can relax.

Chase is this close to being expelled from the prestigious Wellington Academy. Parker, on the other hand, is doing just fine academically—it's her social life that's on probation. When a campus tragedy and a little fate bring Chase and Parker together, Wellington finally starts to make sense to them both. If only it wasn't so easy to mess everything up.

Off Campus

A new year at Wellington means new students, new drama, and the same old rule: Don't get caught.

Nikki is an old pro at the boarding school thing now. She's ready to show someone else the ropes, someone like Delia. A transfer student with a dark past, Delia doesn't quite fit in anywhere, but she sure knows how to have fun. But when fun leads to sneaking off campus, it can very quickly turn dangerous.

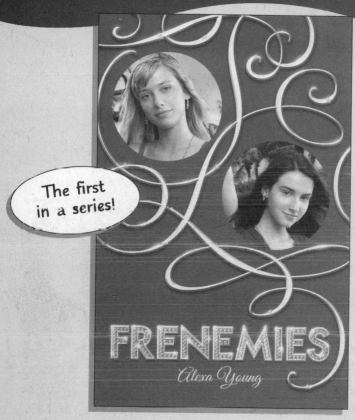

Enjoy HarperTeen hits, now in paperback!

Bittersweet Sixteen
By Carrie Karasyov and Jill Kargman

Balloons and streamers? Carvel cake? That might be standard fare for your average birthday party, but the students at Tate, a posh all-girls Manhattan high school, are anything but average. Now, with everyone tuning in to the all–Sweet Sixteen, all-the-time channel, tempers are flaring and Prada bags are flying. In the end, whose Sweet Sixteen will reign supreme?

Summer Intern
By Carrie Karasyov and Jill Kargman

Kira Parker can't wait to spend her summer in New York City, interning at popular fashion magazine, *Skirt.* She is determined to prove herself to the magazine editors—even if it means pitting herself against the snobbiest of the interns, whose father also happens to own the magazine.

Pretty Little Liars
By Sara Shepard

In the exclusive town of Rosewood, PA, where the sweetest smiles hide the darkest secrets, four pretty little liars—Spencer, Aria, Hanna, and Emily—have been very bad girls. They've kept their scandalous secrets hidden for years, but now someone named "A" has the dirt to bury them all alive.

For Pretty Little Liars gossip, giveaways, and more, visit www.prettylittleliarsbooks.com.

HARPER TEEN
An Imprint of HarperCollins *Publishers*

www.harperteen.com